D0110523

BANANA
SPLITS

LONDON PUBLIC LIBRARY
WITHDRAWN

BANANA
SPLITS

Coco Simon

Simon Spotlight

New York   London   Toronto   Sydney   New Delhi

LONDON PUBLIC LIBRARY

If you purchased this book without a cover, you should be aware that this book is stolen property. It was reported as "unsold and destroyed" to the publisher, and neither the author nor the publisher has received any payment for this "stripped book."

This book is a work of fiction. Any references to historical events, real people, or real places are used fictitiously. Other names, characters, places, and events are products of the author's imagination, and any resemblance to actual events or places or persons, living or dead, is entirely coincidental.

SIMON SPOTLIGHT
An imprint of Simon & Schuster Children's Publishing Division
1230 Avenue of the Americas, New York, New York 10020
This Simon Spotlight edition August 2019
Copyright © 2019 by Simon & Schuster, Inc.
All rights reserved, including the right of reproduction in whole or in part in any form.
SIMON SPOTLIGHT and colophon are registered trademarks of Simon & Schuster, Inc.
For information about special discounts for bulk purchases, please contact Simon & Schuster Special Sales at 1-866-506-1949 or business@simonandschuster.com.
Text by Tracey West
Series cover design by Alisa Coburn and Hannah Frece
Cover design by Laura Roode
Cover illustrations by Alisa Coburn
Series interior design by Hannah Frece
The text of this book was set in Bembo Std.
Manufactured in the United States of America 0719 OFF
10 9 8 7 6 5 4 3 2 1
ISBN 978-1-5344-5213-8 (hc)
ISBN 978-1-5344-5212-1 (pbk)
ISBN 978-1-5344-5214-5 (eBook)
Library of Congress Catalog Card Number 2019942244

CHAPTER ONE
THE QUEEN OF SOCIAL MEDIA

"I need another bird's nest sundae with strawberry ice cream, please!" I called to Allie.

"Bird's nest sundae coming right up!" Allie replied.

I watched my friend make the sundae—one scoop of strawberry ice cream topped with shredded coconut, jelly beans, and a Peep. The result looked like a bird sitting on its eggs in a nest, and I absolutely loved it. It was my latest sundae creation and probably one of my favorites yet.

The customers loved it too. I'd been counting the sales of the new sundae ever since I'd started taking orders at twelve forty-five, and in just two hours we'd sold thirteen of them!

Allie handed me the sundae, which I finished off with a Molly's Ice Cream trademark—a shower of sprinkles.

"Here's your sprinkle of happy," I said with my best salesclerk smile, handing the sundae to the woman who had ordered it. The little girl next to her began to jump up and down in excitement.

"Ice cream! Ice cream!" she shouted.

"Calm down, Sophie," her mom said patiently. "I just need to pay, and then we'll sit down."

I laughed. "It's okay. We all feel that way about ice cream," I told her. The woman gave me a grateful smile and made her way over to pay my friend Sierra at the register.

I spun around to Allie. "Thirteen in two hours!" I bragged.

"I was counting too. That might be a record," she said. Then she scrunched up her freckly nose in that way she does when she's thinking. "I wonder if it *is* a record. Why haven't we ever thought about keeping stats on this kind of thing?"

"We could, if we input flavors into the computer register system," Sierra chimed in, tapping the register. "Right now it only keeps track of small sundae, medium sundae, small cone, things like that."

"This sounds like a job for Sierra Perez, math genius," I said, wiggling my eyebrows.

"That might be beyond my genius capabilities," Sierra answered. "But I'll talk to your mom about it, Allie."

"Awesome!" Allie replied.

Allie's mom, Mrs. S., owned Molly's Ice Cream, which was named after her grandmother. Allie, Sierra, and I had been besties since we were tiny, and we worked together in the shop every Sunday afternoon. I was glad we did, because Allie's parents had gotten divorced the previous summer, and now Allie went to a different school from where Sierra and I went. For most weeks, our Sprinkle Sunday was the only day when we were all together in the same place.

I gazed around at the shop. Three teenage girls were sitting on the stools at the high counter that faced the window. A dad and his two little boys were eating ice cream cones at one of the small round tables, and at the table next to them, Sophie was digging into her bird's nest sundae while her mom watched.

I wiped my hands on my apron. "I'm going to take a few photos for the website while it's quiet," I announced.

3

"Great. I'll refill the toppings," Allie said.

"I'll help!" Sierra quickly offered.

A few months before, Allie might have been upset that I was taking pictures instead of helping with the toppings. But ever since her mom had made me the unofficial social media director of the shop, Allie didn't mind as much. I added all of the updates to the Molly's Ice Cream website. I uploaded photos to the shop's social media accounts, and I responded to any messages or comments people posted. I didn't mind doing it, because Mrs. S. was so busy making the ice cream and keeping the shop running seven days a week that all these things would never get done if I didn't do them. Also, it was a lot of fun!

I walked up to Sophie and her mom. "Would you mind if I took a photo of your daughter with the sundae and posted it on our website?" I asked. "We'll identify her by first name only."

"I wouldn't mind at all!" the mom replied. She pulled a napkin from the dispenser. "I should clean up her face first, though."

"No, it's perfect. Trust me!" I said. Sophie had ice cream all over the outside of her mouth, and flecks of coconut and sprinkles stuck to it. I pointed my phone at Sophie. "Smile and say 'ice cream'!"

"Ice cream!" Sophie cried, scrunching up her eyes. When she opened her mouth to smile, I noticed that she was missing her two front teeth. How cute was that? This was social media gold!

"Okay. Now pick up the spoon and pretend you're going to put it into your mouth, but stop just before you get there," I instructed.

Sophie obeyed, and I snapped away.

"That was great! Thanks!" I said. "You can find the photos on the Molly's Ice Cream website."

Sophie's mom nodded, and then I moved to the dad and his two boys. I took a few shots of them eating their ice cream cones. And the teenage girls let me shoot them sipping their milkshakes with our new paper straws—aqua-colored, to match the cushions on the chairs.

"Wait. Let us see!" one of the girls demanded before I could walk away. I handed them my phone, and they huddled together, scrolling through the photos.

"Wow, these are all good!" the girl said. "You should be, like, a professional photographer or something."

"Thanks. It's part of my job," I replied. I *knew* I was good, but it was nice to hear it from other people.

No new customers had come in, so I went back behind the counter and began to upload the photos. First I posted them to the website, and then to the social media accounts, which were all linked, so I only had to post them once.

For Sophie I wrote: Cute alert! Order a bird's nest sundae, and you'll be smiling too. #SundaySundae #IceCream #MollysIceCream #Bayville #Cute

For the dad and the boys I wrote: Molly's is open till 9 every Sunday! #IceCream #SundaySundae #IceCreamCone #MollysIceCream #Bayville

For the teenage girls I wrote: Milkshakes taste better with our new planet-friendly straws. #Milkshake #SavethePlanet #MollysIceCream #Bayville

I could have come up with at least ten more hashtags, but I heard Allie call out behind me.

"Incoming!"

A group of little girls in soccer jerseys came in with their coach. I slipped my phone back into my pocket.

"On it!" I said, and I turned on the charm with a big smile for the coach. "Welcome to Molly's. How can I help you today?"

The rush lasted for about an hour, but I had a chance to check the social media accounts before our shift ended and it was time to clean up.

"Wow!" I said. "Sophie's photo has forty-five likes online already."

"Who's Sophie?" Sierra asked.

"That little girl who ordered the bird's nest sundae. The girl with the two front teeth missing," I replied.

Sierra nodded. "She *was* cute!"

"Twenty-eight likes on our yummy milkshakes," I reported. "Oh, and here's a comment: 'How late are you open tonight?'"

I rolled my eyes. "Duh. It says right in one of the captions that we're open till nine."

"Don't write that!" Allie warned.

"Of course not. I am the queen of social media. I know exactly what to say," I responded, and then I typed, "Open till 9. Hope to see you soon, and bring a friend!"

Sierra grinned. "The queen of social media, huh? Was there an election?"

"Queens don't get elected. They are born," I pointed out. "And anyway, I am killing it with the website and the other social media accounts. Molly's has a legit social media presence now. Kai says we're on the way to becoming a recognizable brand."

Kai was my business-obsessed older brother. I got a lot of good advice from him.

I checked out another photo of a family eating ice cream cones. "Okay, now here's a sensible comment: 'How come your chocolate ice cream tastes so much better than the kind I make at home?'"

Mrs. S. walked into the room as I was saying this. "Wow, that's flattering. So how do you respond to a comment like that?"

I thought for a minute. "What about this?" I said, and I read out loud as I typed. "Don't even *try* to duplicate it. Why torture yourself and waste time and money trying to make it at home? Life is short! Come to Molly's and enjoy all the best-tasting chocolate ice cream you want!"

Everybody laughed.

"That is perfect," Mrs. S. said. "People tell me they love following Molly's on social media, not just to see what's new but to see 'Molly's' funny responses. You are a star, Tamiko!"

"Actually, she's a queen. Queen of social media," Allie corrected, laughing.

8

"All right. I was just kidding before," I said. "I might be good at social media, but I'm not exactly a star."

"Even kids at school treat you like you're a celebrity," Sierra said.

"No, they don't," I protested.

She turned to Allie and Mrs. S. "People stop by our table at lunch and compliment her on the website. Even *Eeee*-wan," she teased.

I rolled my eyes. Earlier in the year Ewan and I had gotten paired up in art class, and we'd had to draw each other's portraits. I hadn't been exactly psyched about it, because he was a popular kid who hung out with a bunch of jerks. But it turned out he wasn't a jerk. He was nice and a really good artist, and I'd ended up drawing a lot of pictures of him in different styles. So *of course* Sierra and Allie had assumed that meant I had a crush on him, and they'd been torturing me about it ever since.

It was kind of annoying. They were my friends, and I loved them, but just because they were obsessing about boys all the time didn't mean I had to. I had no interest in dating right now. And so what if sometimes my stomach did this weird flip when I passed by Ewan in the hallway. That didn't mean I had a crush on him, all right?

Allie walked over with one of those pointy paper cups that you put your ice cream cone into to prevent drips, and she placed it on top of my head, giggling.

"I crown thee Tamiko, queen of social media!" she said. "What is thy command?"

"I command you to stop calling me the queen of social media," I said, taking the paper cone off my head. "I'm sorry I ever brought it up."

Allie's face got thoughtful. "Tamiko, now that you have a following, you should maybe create a blog of your own. You know, do something more than just post friend stuff on SuperSnap. You could post photos of all the stuff you create."

I liked the sound of that. "I'm not sure why I never thought of that," I admitted. "But I like it. I could post outfits I've made, and get people to rate them and stuff."

"You could even do videos," Sierra suggested.

Mrs. S. nodded. "I think that's a wonderful idea," she said. "It's never too early to start thinking about your future. And a successful website would be a wonderful thing to show to prospective colleges in a few years. That time will be here quicker than you expect!"

"I didn't even think of that," I said. "I love these ideas. Thanks!"

"Now, if you girls don't mind cleaning the tables, I'll get your pay for this week," Mrs. S. said, and she headed to the back room of the shop.

We cleaned up the tables and divided the tips we'd gotten that afternoon. I heard a beep and saw Mom outside in her car.

"Need a ride, Sierra?" I asked. "You can come over for dinner if you want."

"Sounds good, but I can't," she said. "I'm going straight to band practice."

"Cool," I said. "Bye!"

After getting my pay from Mrs. S., I took off my apron and headed outside. Normally, I might have been mildly annoyed that Sierra had band practice—her schedule was so crazy, and she didn't always have time to hang out with me. But that night my mind was whirring with plans.

I couldn't wait to start my blog!

CHAPTER TWO
THE NAME GAME

When we got home, I bounded up to my bedroom.

"Tamiko, come down in twenty minutes and set the table!" Mom called up to me.

"Sure!" I called back.

I would have said that my creative juices were flowing, except I hated that saying. It reminded me of blood flowing through veins, which was gross. So instead I'd have said that I got a . . . creative spark. My mind was bursting with ideas for my first photo shoot.

Themes . . . I can do themes, I thought, rifling through my clothing rack. Not just outfits, but also accessories—stuff that I'd made that wasn't necessarily clothing. I could mix them together in themed photo shoots.

The first thing I pulled out was a maxi skirt I'd created out of a thrift store dress. I wasn't an expert at sewing, but Mom had taught me how to do some basic stuff, like making hems, and this had been an easy project. I'd taken a maxi dress that looked kind of uncool on me and chopped off the top and added elastic around the waist to make it a skirt. The yellow-and-orange pattern looked really summery if you paired it with a white tank top or T-shirt. I hadn't even worn the skirt yet.

I found a white tank top in my drawers and placed it and the skirt on the bed. I could do a "summer's coming" feature and maybe show three different summer outfits and ask people to pick their favorite. But I didn't want to just show the clothes; I wanted to make the shots interesting, maybe pairing the clothing with summer accessories like sunglasses. Or maybe something fun made out of pool noodles. I'd always wanted to craft with pool noodles. . . .

But how would I display the clothes? Should I wear them myself and take mirror selfies? The clothes might look better if somebody were wearing them. I wasn't so sure if I wanted to be the person modeling, but I knew I could probably ask some of my friends to do it. Sierra was great at posing in photos and was also my bestie, so she would be my first choice. But she also had an insane schedule, so I wasn't sure if she was going to say yes.

I was staring at my bed, picturing Sierra in the skirt, when Kai walked into my room.

"Mom wants you downstairs," he said.

"Uh-uh," I replied. I wasn't really listening.

"Well, I can see you're extremely busy working on something important, so I'll just tell her you can't make it," Kai said.

His sarcasm got my attention. "As a matter of fact, this *is* important," I told him. "I'm planning a photo shoot for my new blog."

He raised an eyebrow. "A blog? Great idea," he said. "Which platform are you using?"

To be honest, I wasn't sure I knew what he meant. "I, uh . . ."

"There are some great platforms out there where you can make blogs for free," he said. "They all have ads, but some really bombard you. So you've got to choose carefully."

"I hadn't thought of that," I admitted.

"I can help you with that, if you want," he

offered. "What are you calling your blog?"

I shrugged.

He shook his head. "You're planning a photo shoot, and you haven't even named your blog? That's backward," he said. "First you need to pick a great name that people will remember. Then you need to make sure no other blogs are using that name. Then—"

"Didn't you say Mom wanted me?" I asked, pushing past him.

"Fine. I'm sure other people are interested in free advice from the youngest president of the high school business club in history," Kai said.

I stopped. Kai did know a lot about business, and he'd been really helpful with the Molly's website. It was cool of him to offer to help.

"Sorry," I said. "You killed my creative buzz, but you're right—I need to get the details down first. Can you help me after dinner?"

Kai nodded. "Sure. But once you're monetizing your blog, you're gonna have to start paying me for my services."

"No problem. As soon as I'm a blog millionaire, I'll send you a check," I said, heading down the stairs.

Kai followed me. "Joke if you want. But I can name at least twenty-five kids who became millionaires before they graduated high school. There's Adam Hildreth, who created his own social network in England when he was fourteen. And—"

"Who's creating their own social network?" Mom asked as we entered the kitchen.

"Nobody," I said. "But I *am* going to start my own blog."

Mom nodded. "That makes a lot of sense, I guess. You certainly have a lot to share with the world, Tamiko."

"Unfortunately, she's blog-clueless," Kai remarked. "She was upstairs planning her first photo shoot, and she hasn't even named her blog yet."

Dad looked up from the pan he was stirring on the stovetop. "How about *Sato Says*?" he asked. "I always fantasized about having a newspaper column with that name."

"That's a little corny," I said, grabbing plates from the cabinet.

"And dangerous, Tamiko," Mom said. "I'm okay with you having a blog, but you shouldn't give out your last name online."

"I hadn't thought of that," I said.

"There's a lot of things you haven't thought of," Kai pointed out—again.

I smiled sweetly at him. "Thankfully, my wonderful, nice brother is going to help me figure it out."

"I can give you twenty minutes tonight," Kai said. "Then I've got to study for finals."

"Tamiko, don't get carried away with your blog and forget to study," Mom warned.

"Relax, Ayumi," I said, taking my seat at the dinner table.

Mom sighed. "Honestly, I don't know where you got this idea that it is okay to call your father and me by our first names."

Dad placed a bowl of rice on the table. "Yeah, you had better not let Grandpa Sato hear you do that," he warned.

"I won't," I said. "But I don't think he'd care."

Dad shook his head. "You didn't grow up with him, Tamiko. He is the one who taught me the importance of respect."

"R-E-S-P-E-C-T!" Mom sang.

"Do I have to respect Mom's singing?" I asked.

"No, but you have to listen to it," Mom said with an evil grin.

Then we started piling food onto our plates. Mom cooked most of the time, but Dad said he cooked better Japanese food than she did, since he was born there. Mom didn't argue with him, probably because she didn't want to do all the cooking by herself anyway.

Tonight Dad had made teriyaki tofu, veggies, and rice. I loved how teriyaki sauce was savory but also a little bit sweet.

"I made our flight reservations to Japan today," Mom said. "We're leaving on August 1 and will be back on August 20."

"In time for cross-country practice?" I asked.

Mom nodded. "The schedule's not out yet, but you should be fine."

"I think you should let Hayato and me go into the city alone this year," Kai said. Hayato was one of my cousins.

Mom frowned. "I'm not sure, Kai. I mean, I know you're going to be sixteen, but Tokyo is such a busy city."

"But I'll be with Hayato," Kai said. "He's seventeen, and he goes to school in Tokyo, so he knows how to get around."

Mom looked at Dad. He shrugged. "I think Kai can handle it. I did when I was his age."

I frowned. Every summer we went to Japan to visit Grandpa Sato. He lived in Tokyo. I loved when we visited downtown Tokyo, which was so bright and colorful. It was fun to see what people were wearing on the streets and also the fashions in the shop windows. And to listen to the pop music that you could hear blaring from the shops. I would have loved to go into the city with Kai and Hayato, but I knew there was no point in asking. Even if the boys wanted me to tag along, Mom and Dad would *never* let me.

"You know, when you both were little, I spent weeks planning on how to keep you busy for the summer," Mom said. "But I don't think you need my help anymore with that. Tamiko, Allie's mom might have you in the shop during the week some days, right?"

I nodded. "She's expecting it to get really busy once tourists start coming in the summer," I said. "So Mrs. S. will need some extra help. But she's hiring some more college students too."

"I'm so glad that Allie's mom has made a success

of that place," Mom said. "I mean, she deserves it. That ice cream is *so good*."

"And they've got a great website," I added.

"You should link to the Molly's website on your blog," Kai said. "You know, somebody might be on your page and not even be thinking about ice cream until they see the link and say to themselves, 'Oh yeah, *Molly's*! I should check that place out!'"

I nodded. "That is an awesome idea. I don't know how you do it. Your mind is, like, full of business ideas."

Kai shrugged modestly. "There are more ideas where that came from. Give me a few minutes after dinner, and I'll get a list of some of the best blog hosting sites ready."

"Great!" I said. Despite Kai being kind of annoying earlier, I was feeling really grateful to have a brother with his skills—and excited again to start working on the blog.

After dinner I headed into my room and texted Sierra and Allie.

Need some name ideas for my blog. Go!

Sierra texted back right away. ALL TAMIKO ALL THE TIME! ❤ ☺ ❤ ☺ ❤ ☺

I texted her back with a bunch of laughing emojis.

Allie came through next. She was a good writer, so I wasn't surprised that she had lots of ideas, one after the other.

Time with Tamiko

Tamiko's Fashion Forecast

Flavorful Fashion (Because you work in an ice cream shop. Get it?)

I appreciated Allie's effort, but none of them were quite right. I wanted something simple, and catchy, and . . . fresh, I guess.

Thanks! I need to think about these, I texted back.

Then Kai came in with his laptop, and he showed me the different blog hosting sites.

"I narrowed it down to these two, which are both for bloggers sixteen and under," Kai said.

I frowned. "Wait, what? Am I going to be blogging on a site with a lot of little kids?"

Kai shook his head. "Sixty-seven percent of its users are between the ages of thirteen and sixteen. This is your target audience, Tamiko. Besides, it's smart to go on a safe site like this, where adults can't

21

see your photos or comment on your posts. There are a lot of mean and creepy people online."

I nodded. "All right. You've convinced me. Let me see them."

I spent a few minutes scrolling through the two sites and picked the free one with an easy layout that would allow me to post photos and create polls.

"And you can choose a design for your blog from this list," he said, scrolling to show me. He clicked on one, and a sample page popped up with pink bubble letters and clouds in the background.

"Ooh, cute," I said. "But maybe too pink?"

"Maybe," Kai said. "There are more to choose from." He stood up. "You got this. I'm gonna go study."

"Thanks," I said, not taking my eyes off the screen. The purple design was fun. But ooh, there was a clean black-and-white one with a really cool font. . . .

"Tamiko, it's Grandpa Sato!" Dad called up the stairs.

"Coming, Toshi!" I yelled back.

"Don't push it, Tamiko!" Dad replied, and I bounded down the stairs and into the kitchen, where Dad's laptop was open. Grandpa Sato liked to video-chat with us when he woke up, because here in Bayville it was early evening.

"Ohayō!" I said, which means "good morning" in Japanese. Grandpa practiced his English when he talked with me, and sometimes I practiced my Japanese with him.

"*Ohayō,* Tamiko," Grandpa Sato said.

"How are you?" I asked.

He smiled. "I always wake up happy during baseball season," he said.

Grandpa and I were both big baseball fans, and we spent a few minutes talking about his favorite team, the Swallows. Then he asked me what my plans for the summer were.

"I'm going to keep working at the ice cream shop," I told him. "And also, I'm starting a blog."

"Blog?" he asked.

"It's kind of like a website, but you update it regularly and tell your followers what's new in your life, or post about what you're into," I said. "I'm going to post about all the stuff that I make, I think."

"And people will want to see this?" he asked.

I laughed. "I hope so, Ojiichan!"

"That is very interesting," Grandpa Sato said. "I think you should blog about baseball. I would like to see that."

"Maybe I will. I haven't figured it out yet," I said. "I don't even have a name for my blog yet."

"Whatever you decide to call it, it will be wonderful, Tamiko," he said. "I am sure it will be a big hit. You always have your own special take on everything."

As soon as he said that, it hit me. "*Tamiko's Take*! That's it! That's the perfect name for my blog."

Grandpa smiled. "I like it."

"Thanks, Grandpa!" I said. "Hey, do you mind if I go work on that now? I want to see if the name is taken."

"Get busy!" Grandpa said. "I will talk to you tomorrow morning. Let me finish talking to your father now."

I almost called out "Toshi!" but I stopped myself. The last thing I wanted to do was upset Grandpa after he'd helped me out so much. Instead I yelled out "Dad!" and then ran back up to my room.

Tamiko's Take was going to be the best blog ever!

CHAPTER THREE
AWKWARD

The idea to start my blog had given me the inspiration to start playing with something else—a drawing app on the new tablet I'd bought with some of my Molly's wages. I had resisted the idea for a long time, because there was something about the sound of a pencil scratching on a sketch pad that I really liked. Besides, using a pencil and paper just felt more open and free to me somehow, and I was worried that maybe I wouldn't be able to do as much with a drawing app.

But then I started watching videos of people using the app to draw, and I saw some of the amazing things they could do, like adding glittering effects or quickly changing the size of something. It also looked really easy to revise something when you didn't like what you'd done. One article I read said that professional illustrators were drawing digitally more than ever before, so I thought I should give it a try. Sometimes I thought I might want to go to art school after high school, and I wanted to be totally prepared if I did.

Sketching a logo for *Tamiko's Take* seemed like a good place to start testing out the app. I thought that putting two capital *T*s together might looking cool. I started by using *T*s from different fonts (the app let me do that), but I wasn't crazy about any of them. Then I spent time drawing letter *T*s—some straight, some with lots of curlicues—until my eyes were drooping, and then I went to sleep.

I woke up with more ideas in my head. I slipped my tablet into my backpack so that I could work on the logo during school. Since the school year was almost over, we had a lot of study sessions—or what most kids used as free time. While other kids were talking and goofing around, I could work on my logo.

The morning sun streamed through my bedroom window, and the sky was so bright and blue outside that I definitely felt like summer was here. I took a shower, and then, inspired by the beautiful day, I put on a T-shirt I had bought in Tokyo the previous summer, white with a wood-block print of pink flowers on it. I paired it with striped pants and bright pink sneakers. And after I pulled my hair back into a ponytail, I added some pink hoop earrings for good measure.

I worked on my logo on the way to school and during homeroom, because after the Pledge of Allegiance and announcements, Ms. Zajak let us do whatever we wanted for five minutes, as long as we did it quietly.

My friend MacKenzie leaned over and looked at the tablet.

"*Tamiko's Take*? What's that?" she asked.

"I'm going to start a blog," I said. "It was Allie's idea, actually. Since the Molly's website is so popular."

"That sounds like fun," MacKenzie said. "I'd read your blog."

"Thanks!" I said. "I'll send you the link as soon as it's up."

The bell rang, and I resisted the urge to draw and walk at the same time. The last time I hadn't resisted, I'd ended up walking into a wall, which was totally embarrassing. So I put my tablet away and rushed to the art room, hoping that Mr. Rivera would let us draw whatever we wanted. But of course the chances were slim, because he was such a boring teacher.

Taking my seat in the art room, I got a sudden inspiration from all of the wood tables in there. I could make my *T*s look like tables! I sketched the first one with DIY fashion stuff on it: feathers, a glue gun, a hat with a crocheted flower on it, and a spool of thread. On the other table I drew an ice cream sundae with two scoops and a cherry. Then I drew some more ice cream treats: an upside-down cone in a cup, and a banana split. It looked busy, but this design was my favorite so far. I couldn't wait to show Allie and Sierra and see what they thought!

"Ms. Sato, are you aware that the bell has rung?"

I flipped over my tablet and sat up straight at the sound of Mr. Rivera's voice. Today he was wearing a boring white shirt and the same boring blue tie he'd worn Friday. Couldn't he at least wear a striped tie? And what kind of art teacher wears a tie to begin with? I'd always thought artists were supposed to be free-spirited and creative, but Mr. Rivera's spirit was more like a bank teller's.

"Sorry, Mr. Rivera," I said.

He nodded. "For our last project of the year, I'd

like you to choose a famous building or structure and draw a detailed sketch of it," he said. "This will exercise some of the skills you've developed this year, such as perspective and shading."

Pete Bradley's hand shot up. "What do you mean, a structure?"

"The Brooklyn Bridge. The Roman Colosseum," Mr. Rivera said. "I want to encourage you all to select something challenging. A skyscraper rather than a shed. I'd like to see you give some attention to the architectural details of your subject. You may use your phones to find a reference, but if I catch anyone texting, your phone will be confiscated."

Mr. Rivera could not have given a more boring description of the assignment, but I was excited anyway. I knew exactly which building I wanted to draw, and I did a quick search for it on my phone as soon as Mr. Rivera stopped talking.

The Chrysler Building was a skyscraper located in Manhattan in New York City. It was built in the art deco style in the 1920s.

I knew about art deco, no thanks to Mr. Rivera. Mom had found a book about it at a yard sale the previous summer and had gotten it for me. Art deco was a style of art created in France, and there were tons of examples of buildings, jewelry, and other objects with a modern look and beautiful, clean shapes, made of really gorgeous materials like shiny metals and gleaming glass. The style was glamorous and cool.

One of the things that made the Chrysler Building art deco was the shape of the spire at the top—half circles one on top of the other, decorated with triangles. I stared at the photo on my screen. A tall, straight tower rose up in between two buildings that anchored the tower on the bottom. What looked like hundreds of windows covered each side of the building. It was going to take a lot of work to get it right, but I knew that this level of detail was going to impress Mr. Rivera for sure.

In art class we used the same sketchbook for the whole year, so all of our work would be in one place. I opened up mine, which was almost completely filled after a year of sketching. The last drawing I'd done was of a boy with spiky dark hair and a dimple in his left cheek . . . Ewan, the boy Allie and Sierra loved to pointlessly tease me about.

I flipped through my book to the first sketches we'd done of buildings, trying to remember what we'd learned. Looking at the Chrysler Building photo, I had a feeling I'd need to use a ruler. Not my favorite way to draw, but I wanted to get this right, and I saw a few other kids getting out their rulers too. Then I connected my phone to the classroom printer and printed out the photo I'd found.

With all of my tools in place, I got to work. I used the ruler to figure out how wide the tower was compared to the two lower parts of the building on either side, and how tall it was. I made some guidelines in my sketchbook and then started on the beautiful curved top of the building. I could have saved it for last, but I wasn't one of those people who saved the best for last. When I ate an ice cream sundae, I ate the cherry on top first. (It helped that I worked in an ice cream shop, because I could always grab another cherry to eat at the end if I wanted. But that was beside the point.)

Getting the size of each curve just right was challenging, and I was concentrating really hard when I heard a voice behind me.

"Great choice!"

I shrieked, and everybody around me laughed. I turned around to see that the voice belonged to Ewan and, thankfully, not Mr. Rivera.

"Sorry," Ewan said, laughing. "Actually . . . not sorry. That was pretty funny."

I had to admit that he was right, and I laughed too. "I was just really into my sketch," I told him. "I didn't even realize you were behind me." I held up my sketchbook. "What do you think?"

"Nice!" Ewan said. "I always liked the Chrysler Building too. It's so art deco and cool."

I tried not to show how impressed I was that he knew about art deco. "So what are you drawing?" I asked him.

Ewan laughed again. "We were close," he said. "I also chose a New York landmark building."

He held up a sketch he had started of the Empire State Building. "But now I don't know," he said. "Too boring? Should I add a little King Kong scaling up the side?"

"That would be hilarious!" I replied. "I'm not sure how Mr. Rivera would feel about it, though. But I think the class would love it."

Ewan grinned and closed his sketchbook. "That settles it! I'm going to do it. It's the end of the year, so I might as well live dangerously," he said. "Worst case scenario, he makes me take it out."

Then he kind of coughed a little bit. "By the way . . . are you going to the block party over on Wilson Street next weekend? I heard that the band your friend is in, the Wildflowers, will be performing."

I nodded. "Yes! Sierra is so psyched that they booked a second gig. I'm definitely going."

"Oh, okay. Because I'm going too," he said, and then he did that strange cough thing again. "And I was wondering if . . ." He hesitated for a minute, and then a thought hit me and I panicked. *Oh no, I* thought. *Is he going to ask me to go with him?*

Ewan got a weird look on his face then, and he might have noticed my panicked look. I was definitely not good at hiding my emotions.

"I was just wondering if you were going to be there," he said, and I saw that his cheeks had gotten a little bit red. "So I guess I'll see you there, then."

"Yeah, I guess you will," I said, and the awkwardness between us right then was as thick as peanut butter. I knew I had to change the subject. "Hey! If I had a blog, would you check it out?"

Ewan gave a little sigh of relief. "Sure, why not? Where can I find it?"

"It's not up and running yet," I said. "But it's close.

I'm going to call it *Tamiko's Take*. I'll let everyone know when it's live."

"Cool," Ewan said, and then he glanced over my head. "Okay. I see Mr. Rivera giving me the stink eye. I'd better get back to my seat. Talk to you later."

He hurried away, and I couldn't help wondering, *Was he about to ask me to the party? Why did I panic when I thought he was going to? Would it be so terrible if he had asked me?*

I could talk to Sierra and Allie about it later—or maybe not. They were always teasing me about Ewan, even though I'd said a *million* times that I didn't have a crush on anybody and I wasn't ready for anything like that.

It was all too much to think about, so I returned to my drawing. I had hundreds of tiny windows to draw, so I started on them. After my forty-seventh window my mind was empty of all thoughts except windows.

I guess that was one reason why I liked art so much. It calmed my mind when I had a lot on it. And between planning the blog and figuring out the whole Ewan thing, my mind was pretty full!

CHAPTER FOUR

MY FIRST PHOTO SHOOT

I became totally obsessed with my blog. On Monday night I texted my logo design to Allie and Sierra and got their feedback.

So cute! 😊 Sierra responded.

Does it have to be 2 Ts? Allie asked. Maybe just one T for Tamiko. And put both the 🍦 and 🎣 on it.

BRILLIANT! I texted her. I immediately got to work on revamping the logo. It definitely looked less busy the way Allie had suggested. I did the big *T* that looked like a table, followed by "Tamiko's Take." Thanks to the app, I could easily upload the logo to my blog layout, and it looked really good in place.

Now I just needed something to post. I opened

my closet and pulled out the maxi skirt I'd made and held it up to me, looking into the mirror. Once again I wondered if I should model it myself. I hated the idea of mirror selfies, so I'd have to find someone to take the pictures for me. I could photograph the clothes without anybody in them, but that was boring. All of the best fashion blogs used models. I'd just have to ask Sierra.

I picked up my phone to text her and saw that it was almost midnight! I'd gotten so carried away that I hadn't realize how late it was, and I had to wake up at six to get to school on time.

School was very unfair to artists, I thought. How was anyone supposed to be able to explore their creative talents when every day was so tightly scheduled? I'd been making stuff since I was little, and I knew that when creative inspiration struck, I had to follow it, or I'd lose it.

I got ready for bed, thinking about what life might be like if I became an artist in the future. I'd have a cute little apartment by the beach, or maybe even in a city like New York or Tokyo. I'd have a whole room for my art studio, and I could stay up all night creating things, playing music as loudly as I wanted. . . .

"Tamiko? Don't you hear your alarm?"

I woke up the next morning with Mom shaking me awake and my phone alarm going off. I'd been sleeping so deeply that it hadn't woken me up!

I hurried to get ready for school, showering and throwing on black leggings, a black top, and black sneakers, since there was no time to coordinate one of my trademark colorful outfits. At least this way I knew everything matched.

Of course, when I went downstairs, Mom had something to say about my look.

"Tamiko, have you gone goth all of a sudden?" she asked.

"Black is classic," I told her. "You don't have to be goth to wear black."

I grabbed some yogurt out of the fridge and granola from the cabinet and sat down at the kitchen table to mix it together. As I ate, I checked the Molly's Ice Cream website and all of the social media feeds, which I had forgotten to do the night before. I tried to check them every day, because people got an "unfavorable" opinion of businesses that didn't answer questions quickly. That was what Kai had told me.

Since Sunday there were five people who had tagged #MollysIceCream in posts, showing pictures of themselves eating it. I switched from my personal accounts to my Molly's Ice Cream account and liked all of the posts. Then I responded to them all the same way.☺🍦 Thanks for coming! Hope we see you again soon!

Two people had submitted questions to the website. The first one was pretty common: Molly's Ice Cream is the best in the area! My family and I love to go there. What new flavors are coming out?

I replied: Thanks for being a Molly's fan! Our list of new summer flavors will be coming out soon. Check the website for the update!

Then I opened the next question. Do you make ice cream cakes? I'd love a Molly's ice cream cake for my son's birthday.

That one I'd have to ask Mrs. S. about. I didn't think she made ice cream cakes, but maybe she'd want to. I'd have to send her an e-mail and ask.

"Tamiko, don't be late!" Mom warned.

I jumped up from my seat. "Relax, Ayumi!" I said.

Mom shook her head. "Honestly, if I'd ever spoken like that to my mother, I wouldn't be sitting here to talk about it."

"Of course you would," I said. "Grandma Sasaki is the coolest."

I knew Mom would have an argument for that, but I darted out the door before she could give it. When I got to school, I ran into Sierra as we both made our way to the front steps.

"Sierra! What are you doing after school today?" I asked.

"Student council meeting," she replied.

"Student council? But it's the end of the year," I said. "What more is there to do?"

"It's our end-of-the-year review meeting," Sierra said.

"Wow, you guys love to have meetings," I remarked.

Sierra nodded. "Tell me about it."

"Okay. Then what about tomorrow after school?" I asked.

"Band practice," she replied. "We've got that block party coming up."

I frowned. "Do you have any time in your schedule? Because I need a model for my blog, and you'd be perfect."

"Wow, that sounds like fun," Sierra said, and then *she* frowned. "But between studying for tests, and

39

band practice, and everything else, I'm pretty busy. Can it wait until after school is out?"

I sighed. "I guess," I said. "I'd really love to get the blog out sooner. But I can wait . . . unless . . ." I squealed. "Sierra, I have the most awesome idea! What if I use the Wildflowers for my first photo shoot? You'd be doing me a favor, and it would be good publicity for the band too!"

Sierra's eyes got wide. "Hey, that is a really good idea," she said. "But how would that work? Would you bring the clothes to band practice tomorrow?"

"I can bring clothes, and some accessories, too," I said. "Ask Reagan and Kasey and Tessa if I can have their sizes, and tell them to wear what they normally wear. They all dress pretty cool anyway."

"I haven't even asked them if they want to do it yet," Sierra said.

"Well, ASK!" I was almost shouting in my excitement. "Text them now."

Sierra folded her arms in front of her and gave me a silly grin. "I think you need to say 'please.'"

I pressed my palms together. "Pretty please with sprinkles on top!"

She laughed. "Okay. I'll text them. But I have no idea if they'll say yes or not."

"They will!" I said. "I know they will!"

They did say yes. And that was why on Wednesday I was stuffing Mom's car with a suitcase and two big shopping bags the minute she got home from work.

"Tamiko, are you moving out?" Mom joked.

"Haha," I replied. "Actually, I have a lot of looks I want to try out, and I need to experiment and see what works best together."

"Well, just don't take too long," Mom said. "It's a school night."

"I'll work fast," I promised.

Mom kept pressing me during the car ride. "What's your homework situation?"

"No homework," I said. "I've just got to finish my last project for art by Monday. I have an English paper due tomorrow that I have to proofread. Then I have a social studies test on Friday, and math and science classes on Monday."

"That's a lot of work, Tamiko," Mom said. "Are you sure you should be working on the blog now?"

"They give us plenty of study time at school," I

told her. "And I've been getting good grades all year. I'm good."

"I want you to study tonight when you get home," Mom said. "Promise?"

I crossed my heart. "Promise," I said.

We pulled up in front of Reagan's house—she was the drummer of the band—and could hear music coming from the driveway. I lugged my suitcase and bags out of the car, and Mom drove off.

"No filter on me. What you see is what you get," Sierra was singing as I made my way down the driveway. The Wildflowers had what I guess you'd call an indie rock sound, and Sierra had a really awesome voice. Considering they'd only been performing together for a few weeks, I thought they sounded great.

The sound ended with three loud beats on the bass drum. Sierra put her microphone into the stand and grinned at me.

"Hey, Tamiko!"

"Hey!" I said. "You guys sounded great."

"Thanks," Tessa said as she took her guitar off her shoulders. "I'm trying out some new lyrics."

Reagan stepped out from behind the drums. "So,

what is this photo shoot for again? Some kind of blog?"

"Yeah. I'm starting a blog of, like, fashion and DIY and ice cream and stuff like that," I explained. "*Tamiko's Take*. And I think you guys would be great models for my first post."

Reagan nodded. "Yeah, awesome! Why not? We can use all the exposure we can get."

Kasey, the keyboardist, stood up. "It all depends on what you're going to make us wear," she said. "We don't want to look too different from how we normally do, you know?"

"No, don't worry. I know your styles pretty well," I said. "I brought some things you can wear if you want, or we can just add some accessories to what you're wearing."

I looked at Kasey. She was wearing jeans, as usual, and boots, and a T-shirt of some band called Sleater-Kinney. She wore a short Afro, and the tips of her dark hair were dyed blond. I opened the suitcase and pulled out a black T-shirt with a skull on it that I'd transformed into a cute tank top.

"Since it's a summer photo shoot, what do you think of this?" I asked. "You can still wear your jeans and boots."

Kasey looked pleasantly surprised. "Cool! Can I keep it when I'm done?"

"Sure," I said. I'd found the shirt in a thrift shop and I'd liked it, even though it wasn't exactly my style.

Then I handed Sierra the orange-and-yellow maxi skirt and tank top that had inspired my idea for a summer-themed blog post. "Can you try this on?" I asked.

"Pretty!" Sierra replied, taking it from me.

"You can use my bedroom," Reagan said. "Come on. I'll show you."

Reagan led Sierra and Kasey inside. I turned my attention to Tessa, who had long dirty-blond hair and a kind of laid-back look, with skinny jeans and a flannel shirt that she'd cut the sleeves off of, over a tank top.

"I have just the thing for you," I said, and I brought out a lightweight, baggy blue sweater that'd I'd altered by cutting out the shoulders to create the "cold shoulder" look. "What do you think? Would you wear this over your tank top?"

"Sure, but is it summery?" she asked.

"It's perfect for nighttime at the beach," I replied.

Tessa grinned. "Yeah, I could see that."

Reagan came back out, and I was excited to show her what I'd brought for her. She had dark red hair and freckles, and she always looked really polished and model-y. (Was that a word? "Modelesque"? "Model-icious"?) Anyway, I'd picked out this long red-and-white-striped dress that had had a ruffled bottom and weird little cap sleeves, but I'd chopped the bottom and the sleeves off, and now it was a chic dress. I added some sunglasses that I'd hot-glued with some plastic cherry charms from the craft store, because cherries were in this year. Or at least *Teen Trend* said they were.

"This is really cute," Reagan said. "But I don't think my flats will work with this." She looked down at her black shoes.

I reached into a bag and handed her a pair of white flats. "These are a size six, but they're stretchy. They should fit. And it's only for a few minutes."

"Okay. I'll try them," Reagan said, and she disappeared into her house.

After a few minutes they all came out wearing their new outfits. I added some more accessories—a necklace for Sierra, some bracelets for Kasey and Tessa—and then started taking pictures with my phone. Luckily, it was a sunny day and the light was great for picture taking.

"So, how do you want us to pose?" Sierra asked.

"I, uh—I haven't thought that far ahead," I said. "Maybe we can start with you guys playing your instruments?"

Everybody got back into band practice position. I held up the phone.

"Awesome!" I said. "Why don't you play that song again? And I'll just walk around and take some pictures."

Reagan counted off behind the drums. "One, two, three!"

They launched into the song. I took a photo of the whole band, and then I started walking around to each of them and snapping pictures. I started with Reagan behind the drums, who had this really cool look of concentration on her face. I took a bunch of shots. Then she noticed me and broke into a very professional-looking smile, which I didn't really like. But I took a few of those shots anyway.

Sierra burst out laughing when I started taking her picture, but she composed herself and I snapped away. I knew that some of the pictures were going to look weird, with her mouth wide open, but I could tell that some of them were going to be awesome too.

I shot Kasey playing the keyboard, and Tessa playing the guitar, her long hair hanging across her face. I got a few shots of the whole band together before the song was over.

"That was awesome!" I said. "I liked the song. And the pictures came out great."

"Can I see?" Sierra asked, looking over my shoulder.

"I took so many!" I said, worried that she and the others might start telling me which photos I should use and which ones I shouldn't. "I promise, I'll only pick flattering ones for all of you."

I turned to the other girls. "Can I take some posed pictures now?"

Kasey jumped out in front of her keyboard, put one hand on her hip, flashed a peace sign with the other, and stuck out her tongue. "Like this?"

I laughed. "Perfect!" I said. The other girls got into it too, and I got some cool shots of Tessa with her guitar, Sierra leaning against the garage and looking to the side in a really dramatic way, and Reagan in front of her drum kit.

It's funny how people react to having their picture

taken. Sierra was at ease in front of the camera, no matter what I asked her to do. Tessa was great in candid shots, but the minute I asked her to pose, she froze up and looked really uncomfortable. I had to keep talking to her while I took her picture to keep her at ease. Reagan was fine, but she lit up when she was behind her drums. Her face just glowed in the shots I took of her behind her drum set. And Kasey was the most anxious one—she must have asked me a hundred times if she looked okay. Meanwhile she was the most photogenic of the group! She looked amazing at every angle. I was feeling great. I knew that I'd gotten some great shots of everyone.

Then I heard a horn beep—it was my dad, coming to pick me up.

"I gotta run!" I said. I started shoving stuff back into my bags.

"Do you want us to change out of the clothes?" Reagan asked.

"Keep them for now," I said. "I can get them back from Sierra sometime."

"But I still get to keep the T-shirt, right?" Kasey asked with a grin.

I smiled back. "Of course!"

I ran to the car and put the bags into the back seat.

"Hey, Dad!" I said, climbing into the front seat.

"Looks like a big production," Dad said, glancing at the bags in the back.

"Yeah. I guess I'm pretty excited about this blog," I told him.

"You are getting more and more like Kai," Dad said.

I gasped. "You can't be serious! Kai is all business. I'm the creative one."

"Ah, but Kai's business ideas are very creative, aren't they?" Dad pointed out. "And you are using your creativity to promote the ice cream shop, and to create your own brand. Those are business skills."

I hated when Dad was right. "Well, maybe, but I still think Kai and I are pretty different," I said. "If you ever catch me wearing a polo shirt, call the doctor."

Dad laughed. "Well, you are funnier than Kai, that's for sure," he said. "But don't tell him I said that."

"I don't have to tell him," I said. "What you said is a well-established fact!"

Mom had made dinner that night, and I ate quickly so that I could go up to my room and work on my blog. But when I stood up from the table, Mom held out her hand.

"Uh, if you're doing a high five, your hand's in the wrong place," I said.

"Please give me your phone," Mom said. "You can have it back after you proofread your English paper and study for your test on Friday."

I sighed. "Fine, Ayumi," I said, handing over the phone. I knew I couldn't argue with her, but at least I could annoy her.

I went up to my room and proofread my English paper. Then I read over my social studies study sheet and wrote notes while I did it, to prove that I'd been studying. When I finished both, I found Mom and showed her.

"Phone, please," I said.

Mom put on her reading glasses and looked over all of the papers I'd given her. "Looks good, Tamiko. Just please don't stay up too late. School will be over soon, and then you'll have plenty of time to work on your blog."

"That's part of the reason why I'm anxious to get it started," I said. "I want the blog to go live while I'm still in school, so I can get feedback from everyone."

Mom nodded. "I get it. Just don't skimp on the studying, okay?"

"OKAY!" I promised in the most exaggerated tone I could muster. I started swiping my screen on the way back to my room and found a text from Allie.

Heard you had a photo shoot with the Wildflowers today. How'd it go?

I got a sinking feeling as I stared at the text. I hadn't invited Allie to the photo shoot, or asked her to be a model. I didn't think it was a big deal, except for the fact that she maybe (definitely) liked this boy Colin in her school, and Colin maybe liked her back or maybe liked Tessa from the Wildflowers. Allie wasn't really sure. I was guessing that Colin wasn't sure either. Had I been a bad friend by not including Allie?

I immediately had an idea. I knew I wanted to work ice cream into my blog somehow, the way that Allie recommended ice cream flavors to go with the book reviews in her school paper. I still needed to ask Mrs. S. if I could link my blog to the Molly's website. Maybe I could go down to the shop the next day and photograph some ice cream to go with my photo shoot of the Wildflowers. I could take photos of some summery ice cream sundaes and get Allie to pose with them.

Great! I typed back. Are u at the shop tomorrow?

Yes.

I need u to model for me. Wear ur Molly's T-shirt.

📷 😃 I'm in!

🌙 Good night! CU tomorrow!

I flopped onto my bed, tired. I wanted to go to sleep, but I was really anxious to look through the photos I'd taken and choose some for the blog. I also wanted to come up with a sundae idea for the shoot at Molly's the next day.

Aspiring to be the queen of social media for real was turning out to be exhausting!

CHAPTER FIVE
GOING LIVE!

"Ali-li! You look adorbs," I said when I walked into Molly's the next afternoon.

Instead of her usual messy ponytail, Allie's brown hair was in a long side braid, and she wore a blue headband that perfectly matched her Molly's T-shirt.

Her cheeks turned pink underneath her freckles. "Well, since you're taking pictures today, I thought . . ."

"You look great!" I said.

"So, how do you want to do it?" Allie asked. "What kind of ice cream do you want in the shot?"

"I came up with an idea for a Wildflowers sundae," I said. "You wouldn't have to sell it in the shop, but I thought it would be fun for the shoot. If you let me make it, I'll pay for it."

Allie's mom was behind the counter, making an ice cream for a customer. She nodded to me. "If it's publicity for Molly's, then it's on the house," she said.

"Thanks, Mrs. S.!" I said. "I've been meaning to ask you if it's okay if I link to the Molly's website from my blog."

"Of course," she replied with a smile. "Anything to get traffic to the site. And you can put your blog on the Molly's website too."

"Wow, I didn't even think of that! That would be great, since Molly's already has so many visitors. Thanks!" I said. Then I put on an apron and washed my hands. "Just give me a minute, Allie, and after I make the sundae, I'll take some shots of you holding it up."

Allie nodded and went back to filling the napkin dispensers. I got to work making a sundae. One scoop of Lavender Blackberry ice cream, because lavender is a flower. (Wildflowers. Get it?) I squirted some whipped cream on top. Then I began to carefully cut into some strawberries to make them look like flowers. I'd seen a video of it, and it wasn't that hard. I just made rows of tiny cuts all around the strawberry to look like petals. Then I placed five strawberry flowers on top of the whipped cream and added purple and pink sprinkles.

"That's very pretty, Tamiko," Mrs. S. said. "They're definitely too time consuming to do every day, but I could see doing them for Valentine's Day or Mother's Day."

"Those are great ideas," I said. "We could make the strawberry flowers in advance, so making the sundaes would go more quickly."

"Let me see," Allie said, coming behind the counter. She smiled. "Very pretty! That's definitely a Wildflower sundae! Sierra's going to love it."

"Why don't you pick it up," I said, "and just hold it up, right here, with your back to all of the flavors in the freezer?"

Allie obeyed. "How's this?" she asked.

"Perfect!" I said, and I started to take pictures. "Just raise your head a little bit and smile. Now look at the sundae. Perfect!"

"I should get a photo of you making one of the strawberry flowers," Allie suggested. "You know, so your readers can see how you did it."

I nodded. "I should have thought of that. Thanks, Allie!"

55

I gave her my phone, and she got close-ups of my hands as I cut a strawberry to make it look like a flower.

"This is perfect," I said, scrolling through the pictures. "Thanks so much, Allie! Thanks, Mrs. S.!"

"Now, don't let that sundae go to waste," Allie's mom said. "Eat up, you two!"

Allie and I each grabbed a spoon and settled down at one of the tables to eat the sundae.

"Mmm, good," Allie said after her first bite. "I'm thinking it might be even nicer with some kind of syrup. Strawberry syrup, maybe? Or some other kind of berry?"

"Definitely," I agreed, and then I felt a moment of panic. "Should we redo the shoot?"

"I think it's fine for the shoot," Allie said. "The Wildflowers will love it. The publicity is good timing, with their gig at the block party coming up."

That remined me of what had happened with Ewan. And since Allie and I were besties after all, I decided to tell her about it.

"So, I think Ewan was going to ask me to go with him to the block party," I blurted out, and then I explained the whole thing to her.

Allie's eyes got wide, and she nodded. "It definitely sounds like he was going to ask you. What would you have said?"

I shrugged. "I don't know. I am seriously not interested in dating, or whatever. But I like Ewan. He's nice. So I guess it would depend on what it *meant* for us to go to the block party together, right?"

"You mean like if you're just going as friends, or as something more?" she asked.

I nodded. "What would you think if Colin asked you to go to the party with him?"

"I'd think he was asking me because we're friends," she answered. "And because we work together on the school paper."

"Right. But what if he showed up with Tessa? Would you think they were just going as friends?" I asked.

Allie bit her lip. "I guess I would probably think something different." She took another bite of ice cream.

"I didn't mean to—all I'm saying is it's complicated," I said. "If Ewan and I showed up together, people would probably think we were going out, even if we went as just friends. It's so complicated!"

Allie nodded. "But Ewan *didn't* ask you. And Colin didn't ask me. So I guess it's not complicated after all, right?"

I laughed. "Right," I said. "In fact, I know how we can keep things uncomplicated. Will you go to the block party with me?"

Allie smiled. "It's a date!"

I reached for another spoonful of sundae, and my spoon came up empty as I realized we'd hit the bottom of the bowl. This was one of the most in-depth conversations I'd had with Allie since she'd switched schools. I guess that was the power of ice cream!

I stood up. "I'm going to go home and try to finish setting up the blog. That is, if my mom lets me."

"Good luck!" Allie said. "Let me know when it's up, so I can read it."

"Will do!" I said, and then I headed home.

That night was a repeat of the night before. Mom confiscated my phone until I could prove to her that I had studied for my social studies test and worked on my sketch of the Chrysler Building. I spent an hour literally sketching nothing but tiny windows. As beautiful as that building was, I was starting to regret choosing it!

Then I uploaded all of the day's photos to my iPad and focused on my blog. I had my logo—my blog title, *Tamiko's Take*—and then a few lines that described what to expect from my blog.

"Fashion and DIY ideas from my Technicolor mind. With some ice cream for dessert."

Then I titled my first post: "Summer Is Coming, and the Wildflowers Are Blooming!"

I wrote a blurb underneath that. "The Wildflowers are exploding onto the Bayville music scene. They'll be playing gigs all over town this summer. Let's meet the band and check out what they're wearing!"

I posted a pic of Reagan first, because she was the leader of the band, even though she was behind the drums. I explained how I'd made the dress and the cherry sunglasses. I did the same with the rest of the band members.

Then I posted the photo of Allie holding the Wildflowers sundae and wrote, "In honor of the Wildflowers, I made this sundae at Molly's Ice Cream shop in Bayville—Lavender Blackberry ice cream, whipped cream, and strawberries, topped with Molly's trademark sprinkle of happy. Nom, nom!"

I added the photo of me cutting the strawberries.

"Making the strawberries isn't hard. You just need to cut rows of petals," I wrote.

I ended with a photo of the Wildflowers band all together.

"Come see the Wildflowers tear up the Wilson Street block party next weekend! And comment below and let me know how you liked my first blog post. Thanks!"

After that I added a link to Molly's Ice Cream. Then I proofread everything to make sure I hadn't made any mistakes.

It was nine thirty by the time I was ready to go live. I took a deep breath and clicked on Upload My Blog.

I hope somebody reads this, I thought, and then I remembered my promise to Allie. I sent the blog link in a text to her, Sierra, and MacKenzie all at the same time. Finally I went to the Molly's Ice Cream page. There was a question in the Q and A section: "Where do you get your ideas for your great sundaes?"

It was a perfect opportunity for me to link to *Tamiko's Take*! Writing as "Molly," I replied, "Everyone who works at Molly's helps come up with new flavor combinations and sundaes. For a new sundae idea based on a local band, go to *Tamiko's Take!*" Then I added a link to the blog.

I also added a link to the blog inside the navigation bar on the Molly's web page. I tested it, and the link took me right to *Tamiko's Take*. I had to admit, my blog looked amazing!

I put away my tablet and sketched five more rows of windows on the Chrysler Building, for good measure. Right after I got ready for bed, Kai knocked on my door. "Did your blog go live?" he asked.

I nodded. "Yeah, but how did you know?"

"I got a text from Madison, who said her little sister told her that you had a blog," he said. "Word must be getting around."

"Wait. Madison's sister is Alexis, right? She goes to MLK," I said. "So that makes sense."

Kai took control of my tablet. "See this little icon up here? Scroll over it, and then click on Insights," he said. "That keeps track of your visitors in real time."

"Seriously? That's cool," I said, and I clicked on it.

"Wow!" I said. "Two hundred and five hits? It's only been, like, an hour."

"Then your instincts were right," Kai said. "You've got what it takes to get a following on social media.

That is valuable currency in the digital age."

I hugged him. "I'm not sure exactly what that means, but thanks for your help."

"No problem," Kai said. "When you're ready to monetize your blog, I'll help you out—for a cut."

"Of course. I should have figured you'd have ulterior motives," I said, and I ushered him out the door.

I climbed into bed and clicked on Insights again. I had 209 views! I grinned.

Tamiko's Take was turning out to be a hit!

CHAPTER SIX
I'M A CELEBRITY

I woke up before my phone alarm on Friday morning and checked my blog. I'd had 402 views! I had doubled my views since the night before. And there were comments, too. I was itching to read them, but I forced myself to shower and get dressed first. Now that I was getting famous for a fashion blog, I couldn't go out wearing boring black again.

I chose this cute little white lacy dress that fell just above my knees and a pair of sneakers I had painted with this crazy flower design. I added a beaded necklace I'd made at a jewelry-making class at the craft store. I knew that the plain white dress could take some bold accessories, and I loved the final look when I checked myself out in the mirror.

Walking downstairs, I scrolled through my phone, eager to see the blog comments. Most were kind of generic.

"Cute fashions!"

"Great looks!"

"Can't wait to see the Wildflowers next week!"

And some were really specific.

"What kind of glue did you use when you decorated the sunglasses?"

"Do you have instructions for cutting sleeves off from a shirt?"

"Can you make me a dress?"

My head was spinning. This was way more than I'd ever expected.

"Tamiko! Grandpa says good morning!"

I looked up from my phone. I was surprised. Grandpa usually called at night. "Oh, sorry. Good morning, Grandpa!"

"Good morning," he said. "Why is your face buried in your phone so early, Tamiko?"

"My blog went live last night," I replied. "And I got lots of views and comments! I'm just trying to go through them all."

"That is my Tamiko. Everything you do will be a

64

success," he said, and I grinned. I sure couldn't argue with him!

I fixed myself a bowl of cereal and sat down to try to answer the comments. I was about halfway through when I realized that I needed to check the Molly's website too. Reluctantly I switched to the Molly's account and checked for questions.

"What time do you close tonight?"

I rolled my eyes. Seriously? The hours were right on the front page! But I was nice about it.

"We're open till nine p.m. on Fridays. Hope to see you later!"

Then I rushed to school, hoping to have a chance to answer some blog comments before class started. Instead I ended up answering comments IRL. Everybody was coming up to me and asking about the blog!

Well, not *everybody*, but a lot of people. First my friends Kyra, Victoria, and Ruby surrounded me as I approached my locker.

"Tamiko, your blog is awesome!" Kyra said.

Victoria tossed her hair. "If you ever need more models, just let me know."

"How did you guys find out about it?" I asked.

"I saw the link on the Molly's Ice Cream page," Kyra responded.

"And I'm friends with Reagan from the Wildflowers," Ruby responded. "She posted it last night on the Wildflowers web page."

That explains a lot, I thought. Sierra must have forwarded the link to the band, and if each one of them had posted it somewhere on social media, all of their followers would have seen it. Using the Wildflowers for my first shoot had been a stroke of marketing genius! I couldn't wait to brag to Kai about it.

"Well, thanks," I said.

"So, what is your next post going to be about?" Kyra asked.

I hadn't thought that far ahead. But of course, to have a successful blog I'd have to get people to come back. And that meant lots of new content.

"I'm still working on it," I said. "But I promise, it will be even better than the last one."

The girls walked off, and I ran into Sierra on the way to class.

"Thanks for choosing a good picture of me," she said. "It looks really great, Tamiko. I'm so glad you used the band for your first post. We're getting a lot of attention from it."

"No problem," I replied. "It works both ways. I got a lot of views because you guys posted the blog link! Now I just have to figure out a way to keep readers coming back for more."

Sierra grinned. "Just do you. I don't think you'll ever run out of ideas, Tamiko."

At that moment Jenna Horowitz came walking down the hallway toward us. Jenna was one of the most popular girls in school, and she was a genuine fashion plate. The stuff I made could sometimes look DIY and weird, which was fine, because that was my style. But Jenna always looked like she belonged on a magazine cover. That day she was wearing a black-and-white-striped top with a short yellow skirt that I was pretty sure I had actually just seen on the cover of a magazine. She had long wavy brown hair that never looked messy and always looked perfect.

Jenna, for maybe the first time ever, nodded at me.

"I like your blog, Tamiko," she said, and then she kept walking.

I fake-fainted into Sierra's arms. "Did that really just happen?"

"Looks like you're a celebrity," Sierra said.

Then my bubble burst in art class.

"Everyone, please hand in your final sketches," Mr. Rivera announced.

"Wait. What?" I asked without raising my hand. "You said they were due on Monday."

"No, I very clearly said Friday, and today is Friday," Mr. Rivera said to me, and a few people laughed. "I was very clear that the due date for this project was today."

My Chrysler Building was still missing several rows of windows and a few finishing touches. I swore I hadn't heard Mr. Rivera give us a Friday deadline, but I usually tuned out his voice, so I could understand if that was what had happened.

I raised my hand this time and asked, "Can I turn it in on Monday?"

"Yes, but I will be deducting five points off your grade for lateness," he said. He looked around the room. "That goes for anybody who hands in their sketch late."

Points? How do you use points to judge a work of art? I wondered. Sometimes I thought that Mr. Rivera had no soul.

Ewan turned his head and gave me a sympathetic look, and I almost smiled at him before I remembered the block party conversation.

Thank goodness I had a social studies exam that day, because it took my mind off my art class fail and my (second) awkward Ewan exchange. I knew that I'd have to start focusing on finishing up school over the next few days, but at the same time I was blog obsessed.

On Saturday I finished my Chrysler Building sketch, and I thought it looked great. If I were giving it points, I would give it a thousand. After that I got to work brainstorming blog ideas. I tore apart my closet and looked through all of the DIY projects I was working on at home. In my idea notebook I started making lists of ideas.

The next day, at Molly's, I passed my ideas by Allie and Sierra while we worked our shift.

"Going green? Stuff that is recycled but also the color green?" I shot out.

"Maybe better for Saint Patrick's Day. Or Earth Day," Allie countered.

I nodded. "Okay. What about a post on how to

wear scarves? You know, like different ways to tie them . . ."

Sierra frowned. "I think it's already too hot for scarves. Even the kind you're talking about."

"I thought so," I said. "So, how about a tutorial on how to customize your toilet seat?"

Allie laughed. "I don't think the world is ready for that, Tamiko."

I knew Allie was right. But I was starting to worry. Sierra had told me that I'd never run out of ideas. But I was already stuck on an idea for my second blog post!

Then a gray-haired couple walked into the shop.

"Welcome to Molly's. May I take your order?" I asked.

"We will have one banana split, please, and two spoons," the man said. "It's our summer tradition. The first day we come to the beach, we get a banana split."

A banana split was ice cream served on a banana sliced in half lengthwise, but at Molly's we always served the sundae in a dish shaped like a boat. And we put in three scoops of different-flavored ice creams. Then we added three sauces: chocolate, strawberry, and caramel. The whole thing got topped with crushed walnuts, whipped cream, and a cherry—and of course a sprinkle of happy.

"What flavors would you like?" I asked.

"Well, we usually get chocolate, vanilla, and strawberry," the woman replied. "But I see you have so many unusual flavors here. What would you recommend?"

"Hmm," I said, looking at the flavor board. "It depends on how adventurous you feel. If you're not feeling too adventurous, then I would replace the vanilla with our delicious Banana Pudding flavor, to make your banana split even more bananalicious."

"Oh my, that sounds delicious!" the woman replied. "I think that's plenty adventurous."

I turned to Allie. "One banana split with Banana Pudding, chocolate, and strawberry," I said. While she scooped the ice cream, I sliced the banana in half—and then I got an idea.

"Bananas for bananas!" I cried. "Bananas are summery, and I talk about what colors to wear with yellow, and also make some fun banana accessories, and then show how Molly's makes a banana split!"

"That sounds perfect, Tamiko!" Allie said.

"I like it!" Sierra agreed.

And it *was* a great theme for a post, except I didn't

realize how much work it would take to get it together. I didn't have any yellow clothes I could alter, so that meant I needed to take a trip to the thrift shop. And a trip to the craft shop to get supplies for banana-themed accessories. And I still had homework!

It didn't help that Kai made me feel pressured when I got home that night.

"You should be making a new blog post at least once a week, on the same day, so that your readers will know when to expect it," he told me after dinner (when I hadn't even asked for his opinion). "And if your blog is linked to Molly's, you should also post something smaller every day."

"I can't do a new photo shoot every day!" I argued. "Especially when I'm in school."

"You don't always have to post a photo shoot," Kai said. "You're funny, right? So just post what's on your mind."

I hadn't thought about that. I mean, people liked my sense of humor, but would they view or subscribe to my blog to hear it? Was I that good? I decided to give it a try.

Kai had inspired me. That night I found a photo of the Coyotes, a baseball team. The team shirt had olive-green and white stripes, with green trim around the neck and arms. The pants were baggy on everyone who wore them. I played around with comments that I could write.

"This fashion is hazardous to your health."

"It's not easy being green."

"Who designed this, Oscar the Grouch?"

I finally decided on, "*Not* coming to Fashion Week this year: the Coyotes baseball uniform."

I uploaded it and held my breath. I didn't have to wait long for the comments.

😂

"LOL!"

"I would never wear that!"

I grinned. This was great! I was still excited to plan my photo shoot, but I could do funny photos with captions in between.

And that's what I did. During the next week, between studying and taking tests, I posted one photo a day. I kept it simple and funny. With a photo of chicken nuggets from the school cafeteria, I wrote: "School cafeteria says, 'Eat all your nuggets!' Any leftover nuggets will be served in September." That one got a lot of laughing emojis.

Another day, I posted a photo of the school mascot. It was supposed to be a raven, but the costume was ancient, and all of the feathers were falling off. I wrote: "I think the MLK Raven needs some conditioner!" That one got a smiley face from Carrie Preston, the girl who wore the costume.

I wasn't just getting comments online either. Lots of people were coming up to me IRL to tell me how funny I was. Or they had ideas for what I should post. People who almost never talked to me were offering me ideas.

Pete Bradley came up to me during lunch, holding his lunch tray with mac and cheese. "You should take a picture of this, Tamiko," he said. "You could say, like, 'Gross! Is this supposed to be mac and cheese?'"

He looked at me for approval. I didn't have the heart to tell him that he wasn't being funny, so I just said, "Um, yeah, well, I'll think about it."

Katie Phan slid into the seat next to me during study time. "Are you going to post about what a dork Mr. Walker is? I mean, he's the worst teacher, right?"

"I don't think I should be bad-mouthing teachers on my blog," I told her. "Although, off the record, I agree with you."

Connor Jackson stopped me as I was walking home. "You should make fun of how bad the football team at Jefferson is. You could post a photo of them and say, like, 'Ready for the Stupid Bowl.'"

"I don't want to take sides," I said. "And anyway, I'm not really into football."

Connor shrugged and jogged off.

Some of the comments were annoying. But in a way, it was really flattering. It seemed like everybody in school was reading my blog.

I was actually starting to feel like the queen of social media, and I liked it!

CHAPTER SEVEN

BANANAS!

During lunch one day that week, I asked Victoria to be in my banana split photo shoot. Her green eyes got wide.

"Seriously? I would love to!" she said. "I'm thinking about becoming a model, maybe, and this would really help my portfolio. I mean, I'm tall enough, right?"

I'd always noticed that she was one of the tallest girls in our class, but I hadn't thought much about it. "How tall are you?"

"Five-six," she said. "And I'm supposed to hit five-eleven by the time I'm done growing."

"Wow, that is tall!" Sierra said. "You should totally be a model."

Victoria blushed. "Thanks," she said. "I mean,

it'll be fun to do it for Tamiko's blog anyway."

"Can you do Saturday?" I asked. That meant that I could spend Friday night getting ready for the shoot.

"Sure," she said, and I typed "Shoot with Victoria" into my phone. Then I turned to Sierra. "Now I know what it's like to be you. I'm so busy!"

"I think you need to add, like, five more things to your schedule to compete with me," Sierra said with a smile. "But you're close."

"As close as I want to be!" I joked. "This is exhausting!"

In art class Mr. Rivera handed back our graded sketches. Written neatly and circled at the top of the page was the number ninety-five. And then a note: "This would have been a one hundred if you'd handed it in on time!"

I was not going to miss Mr. Rivera, that was for sure.

After art class Ewan walked up to me. "Your Chrysler Building sketch turned out great," he said. "So I guess I'll see you at the block party?"

"Definitely," I said, and this time I didn't blush. I was pretty proud of myself for that!

I stayed up late Friday, painting tiny bananas on a pair of white sneakers. I turned a basic white button-down shirt into a sleeveless shirt and added a cute yellow ruffle detail down the front. Then I sewed an embroidered banana patch onto a pair of jeans.

On Saturday I met Victoria by the beach for the photo shoot. She changed inside the bathroom at Molly's, and I got pictures of her on the boardwalk, with the ocean in the background. Then we went to Molly's, where Allie had prepared a perfect banana split for the shoot. I took pictures of Victoria eating it at one of the tables in the shop. "When you're a famous model, you can tell everyone that you got paid with a banana split for your first job," I joked.

Victoria laughed. "This is awesome, Tamiko. Thanks," she said. "I'm really glad you asked me to do this."

"I think the photos are going to look great," I told her.

"When will you be posting them?" she asked.

"Tonight," I said, hoping I could follow through. "I want to keep the momentum going."

After Victoria changed and gave me back the clothes from the shoot, I noticed that the shop was packed. Allie looked frantic behind the counter, even though the usual Saturday helpers, Rashid and Daphne, were there.

"Need help?" I called over the counter.

Allie nodded. "It's crazy. It's like the weather got a little bit warmer, and everybody came to Molly's!"

I laughed, washed up, put on an apron, and helped until I had to go home for dinner. Mrs. S. was grateful and paid me for my hours, which I hadn't even been expecting.

"You are a lifesaver, Tamiko," she said. "And I know it's been a busy week for you, but do you think you can answer the comments on the Molly's page when you have a chance? I noticed there are a few of them that haven't been answered in a couple of days."

"Sure thing, Mrs. S.!" I promised. I'd fallen behind on checking the Molly's page during my crazy week. "I'll do it as soon as I get home."

But I didn't. I ate dinner, and then I started putting together my blog post. I still had to take photos of the banana sneakers and some banana earrings I had made. At around nine p.m. I put up the new post. Then I posted the link on SuperSnap, and I texted it to Sierra, Allie, and MacKenzie. And this time I included Victoria.

Finally I went to the Molly's website and added a post about the Molly's banana split with Banana Pudding ice cream, and linked to my blog. Perfect! Then I noticed a bunch of new questions in the comments section. Even though I was yawning, I knew I had to answer them before my shift the next day. I'd promised Mrs. S.

I clicked on the first one.

"Is your ice cream gluten free?"

That question got asked a lot, and it was a complicated answer because some flavors had ingredients like cookies in them, or we used cookies as mix-ins. And our cones weren't gluten free.

Then I got a notification that I had received a new comment on my blog, so I switched over to the blog.

"I am bananas for this blog post!" Allie had written.

Next I went back to the Molly's website to work on questions there. I also had to check the Molly's SuperSnap page. But every time I got a notification about my blog, I checked it. I was so curious to see who was reading it and how they felt about it!

Someone had left a comment on the most recent SuperSnap post for Molly's. "I went to your store at ten p.m. and you were already closed. ☹"

I literally face-palmed. Why couldn't anyone read the hours on the website?

"Sorry we missed you!" I typed. "Molly's is open until eight p.m. Monday to Thursday, and until nine p.m. Friday to Sunday. But you can buy pints to store in your freezer in case you get another late-night craving!"

My eyes were drooping, and I kept yawning, but I wanted to finish. Maybe *I* needed some late-night ice cream. I kept switching back from the Molly's site to my blog.

Then a post popped up on the Molly's site from Jodie Thompson, a girl in my grade at MLK. She'd posted a photo of a banana split—a total disaster of a banana split. A food fail if I'd ever seen one. The whipped cream was sliding off the side; she'd added, like, twenty cherries, which was a ridiculous amount; and the chocolate sauce was in one big glob instead of spread out over all three scoops of ice cream.

"Hey, Molly's, what do you think?" she'd asked. I groaned. Did she really think that sundae was photo worthy? I tried to think of a funny way to answer her.

"You call that a banana split?" I typed. "It's more like banana SLOP! Stop trying to do things you don't know anything about, and leave the ice cream making to Molly's!"

Normally I would have reread my comment before posting it. But it was late and I was tired, and I was especially tired of people asking ridiculous questions on the Molly's website.

I closed my laptop and started to drift off to sleep, but I didn't sleep well. I woke up in the middle of the night and started thinking about my reply to Jodie. While I'd thought my comment was funny, calling her sundae a "banana slop" might have been too harsh.

I climbed out of bed and opened the Molly's web page. Then I deleted Jodie's post and my response.

Problem solved, I thought, and then I fell into a deep sleep.

CHAPTER EIGHT
FROM FAMOUS TO INFAMOUS OVERNIGHT

I woke up and stretched the next morning. The sun was streaming through my window; it was a beautiful sunny Sunday. Today was going to be a great day!

I looked at my notifications. Twenty comments on the blog, more than I had ever received! Excited, I opened the blog and scrolled through the comments.

I gasped. One of the comments on my "Bananas" post was a screenshot of the exchange between me and Jodie on the Molly's website. There was her horrible photo, and her comment, and there was my "banana slop" response.

"We know this is you, Tamiko! Wow, how mean!"

I looked at the commenter's handle, but I didn't recognize it.

Some of the other commenters I did recognize as kids from my school.

"That's so mean!"

"I like Jodie. Leave her alone!" That one was from Jenna Horowitz!

"Noooooooo!" I wailed.

I ran into Kai's room. He was awake and sitting at his desk, working on his laptop.

"Kai, I have an emergency!" I said, and I handed him my phone.

He looked at the screen and frowned. "Wow. This is bad."

"I don't understand," I said. "Everybody loves *Tamiko's Take* because I am funny and I tell it like it is. And now everybody is going crazy because I made a little joke about somebody's banana split?"

I jabbed my finger at the photo on the screen. "Look at it! It's a drippy, uneven mess. It IS banana slop!"

Kai laughed. "Maybe so," he said. "But on the internet, people can't get your tone. They don't know if you're joking, being sarcastic, or being downright mean. You've got to be so careful about what you say. Unfortunately, there will always be people who think the worst."

"Maybe," I said, and then I sighed. "Anyway, I already deleted the comment from the Molly's website. I guess I should delete all these comments from my blog too. There's nothing else I can do."

"I think you should put an apology on your blog too," Kai said.

"Wait, what?" I asked.

"If you offended people, I think it only makes sense to apologize for it," Kai pointed out.

"I guess," I said. "But it doesn't seem fair. I need to think about it."

Kai shook his head, laughing. "You're so stubborn, Tamiko," he said. "Just be nice and say you're sorry. For the good of Molly's."

"I told you, I deleted the comment from the Molly's website," I said.

"Yeah, but that screenshot is out there," Kai reminded me. "Who knows where else it's been posted?"

I groaned. "This is a nightmare."

"Look," Kai said. "You're getting more negative comments as we speak."

"So how do I stop them?" I asked. "Should I delete the post? Or block people? Or take the blog offline until this cools down?"

"That's not a bad idea," Kai said. "But you already know what I think. I think you should apologize."

"Yeah, I know that's what *you* think," I said testily. I took my phone from him and stomped back to my room. I regretted asking for his advice.

What should have been a great day was getting off to a terrible start, and it wasn't even my fault! Everybody was overreacting and being *waaay* too sensitive.

Back in my room, I stared at my phone.

"You are a rotten banana!" Connor Jackson had posted.

Connor was the same guy who'd wanted me to call his football rivals "stupid"! How dare he call me a rotten banana. How DARE he!

I scrolled through all the comments again and noticed that Jodie herself hadn't said anything, which I thought was a little odd because this had all started with her post. Maybe she didn't know about *Tamiko's Take*, or she was still sleeping in. Then a new comment popped up. "Who do you think you are? I'm never going to Molly's again!" Uh-oh. It was bad enough for these people to turn against me. Now they were going to turn against Molly's, too? When I had linked my blog to the Molly's website, I'd thought it would only help Molly's. I had been totally wrong.

And I couldn't believe that someone had taken a screenshot of a comment as evidence, as if they were a private detective or something. If I was the queen of social media, these people were total drama queens. Although, I had to admit, I wasn't really feeling like a queen at the moment.

Why did I ever start this blog? I wondered. *What is the point of working hard to entertain people if they're just going to turn on you?*

I went to my settings and clicked on Take Blog Offline.

A warning popped up on my screen. "Do you really want to do this? Your blog will not be visible to the public."

I clicked on Yes.

That would take care of the problem, I was convinced. I would take a break from the blog for a couple of weeks and wait for this to blow over. I needed a break anyway, after the crazy week I'd had.

As I showered and dressed for my shift at Molly's, I briefly wondered if Allie's mom knew about the post. I had deleted it late last night, and I didn't think that visiting *Tamiko's Take* was on her to-do list on a Sunday morning.

I thought about texting Allie and Sierra to see if they had seen the comments, but decided against it. I was going to see them in a few hours, and it would be easier to talk in person. I wondered how they would react. They wouldn't take sides and accuse me of being nasty . . . right?

Everything will be fine, I told myself. *This is going to be a great day after all.*

I was partly right. But before the day got great, it got a whole lot worse. . . .

CHAPTER NINE
CRUSHED!

"Sprinkle Sundays sisters!" I said as I walked into Molly's for my shift. Allie and Sierra were already there. I cupped my hands around my mouth. "Let's get ready to sell ice creeeeeeeeeeeam!" I called out in a voice like a wrestling announcer.

Allie and Sierra looked at me, but they didn't laugh. My stomach sank a little bit. Before I could talk to them, Allie's mom appeared from the back room.

"Was that Tamiko? Oh, Tamiko, good. I'm glad you're here," she said. "Could you please come with me to the back room? I need to speak with you immediately."

She sounded like a teacher, or like my mom when she's mad at me. I glanced at Allie and Sierra again for support. Did they know what was going on?

Allie looked away from me deliberately, and Sierra just looked sad.

Uh-oh, I thought, and I followed Mrs. S. to her office. She sat down at her desk, and I sat in a chair in front of her.

Mrs. S. took a deep breath. "Honestly, Tamiko, I am very disappointed in you," she said. I knew right away that she was talking about the Molly's website post.

"I'm sorry," I said. "I was tired last night and a little cranky. I deleted the comment almost immediately. But I had no idea that people would take a screenshot of it."

Allie's mom was biting her lip while I was talking. She looked so uncomfortable!

"Tamiko, I know you take great pride in your work, and your creativity is second to none," she said. "But I need you to help me understand why you made that comment in the first place. There is no excuse for insulting someone who is simply trying to have fun and create an ice cream treat at home.

Jodie should not be ridiculed because her banana split wasn't up to an ice cream parlor standard."

"I didn't *ridicule* her," I protested. "It was just a silly joke. I make funny comments all the time on my blog, and even on the Molly's website."

"See, that's what concerns me, Tamiko, that you can't see there is a difference between being funny and being hurtful," she said.

I could feel my face getting hot. "But I *do* understand! I deleted the post, remember! I was just really tired last night. I mean, I know you said no excuses, but I *did* jump in and help out at the shop yesterday. So I wasn't on my game last night when I was replying. And you had told me that I needed to respond to the comments quickly."

I felt kind of bad for bringing up how I had helped at the shop, because I had genuinely wanted to help. But I felt like I was on trial and had to defend myself. *Objection, Your Honor! There were extenuating circumstances!*

Mrs. S. sighed. "I appreciate your help, but this tells me that maybe you need to take a break from running the Molly's website. Just for a little while, until things calm down."

Boom! I felt like a giant hammer had crushed me. I imagined myself as flat as a pancake on the chair.

"All right," I said in a tiny little voice.

"The important thing is to limit the damage," Mrs. S. went on. "I'm going to post an apology on the website right now. And in the future, Tamiko, I'd appreciate you being more careful when you comment on someone's work online."

"Uh-huh," I said absently.

"Thank you, Tamiko," Mrs. S. said, which was a signal for me to leave.

I stood up. I dreaded going back out to the shop, to face those looks from Allie and Sierra. It was humiliating. But then anger suddenly rose inside me and crushed those feelings of humiliation.

This isn't a big deal, I thought. *And now Mrs. S. is suspending me? After all I've done to build up her business on social media. This is so unfair!*

The anger pushed me out the door and to the ice cream counter. I tied my apron without looking at Allie and Sierra, took my position, and put on the biggest, fakest smile I could muster.

"Welcome to Molly's. What can I get you today?"

When the rush died down, I didn't take photos to post on social media, like I usually did. I marched over to the mix-ins station, grabbed the meat tenderizer that we used to crush cookies, and began smashing them.

Smash! Smash! Smash!

Sierra walked up to me with a worried expression in her big brown eyes. "Tamiko, are you okay?"

"Do I look okay?" I asked. "Everybody's mad at me for no reason. Even you and Allie."

Sierra shook her head. "That's not true! I'm not mad at you. I know you're not a mean person. I'm just sad that some people think you are."

"I'm not mad either," Allie chimed in. "It's just that my mom is building a business . . . and needs steady customers. . . ."

"Yeah, and she was getting them, thanks to the website," I pointed out, and I smashed some cookies for emphasis. Was Allie *really* going to blame me for ruining the business? "Everybody is making such a big deal out of this, when it doesn't have to be! I even had to shut down my blog because of all the mean comments I was getting. And people are saying *way* worse things about me than I said about that silly banana split."

93

"I'm sorry that's happening to you," Sierra said. "But maybe if you just apologized, people would stop."

"Allie's mom is apologizing on the Molly's website," I said. "The website I am no longer allowed to manage."

"That's good, but an apology on *Tamiko's Take* would be good too," Allie said. "You might not have meant to hurt Jodie or upset anybody, but you did."

I didn't respond immediately and kept smashing the cookies. I was still angry, but I felt the red-hot rage slowly fading away. Finally I sighed. "That's what Kai told me," I said. "I guess it would make sense to do the thing that my brother and my two best friends are asking me to do, right?"

They both smiled. "Uh, *yeah*!" Sierra said.

I groaned. "Ugh! Apologizing is so embarrassing! But I'll do it. I just need to figure out the right thing to say."

"You're the queen of social media. You can figure it out," Allie said with a grin.

"You also need to figure out what do with all those crushed cookies," Sierra said. "I hate to tell you, but the mix-in jar is already full."

I looked at the crushed-cookie jar. Sierra was right. It was already filled to the brim. In my burst of anger I hadn't even stopped to check if we actually needed a refill!

"Guess I have to promote our cookie-crumble sundae today," I said. We all laughed, and I felt the anger float away. Thank goodness! I hated that feeling. I decided that I was not going to let this whole blog mess spoil my day.

"So does this mean you're still my date to the block party?" I asked Allie.

"Of course!" she replied.

I grinned back. "Awesome," I said, and then the bell on the door jingled and a small party of people came in.

"Incoming!" I yelled, and I ran back to my station by the counter. "Welcome to Molly's. What delicious ice cream treat can I get for you today?"

I felt slightly less crushed to know that Allie and Sierra were mostly on my side. But Allie's comment about me hurting the business had really stung. At first I held my breath, worried that one of the customers would complain about the comment or declare their boycott of Molly's. No one seemed to know about the comment, though, or even the apology that Allie's mom had probably posted by now. As I took order after order, I thought, *If people are still coming to the store, what does it matter if I apologize on my blog or not?*

Ugh. Well, I had promised my friends that I would apologize. And I would. But I was going to do it on my terms, in my own sweet time.

CHAPTER TEN
PARTY TIME!

The Wilson Street block party always took place during a three-day weekend. Wilson was the longest street in Bayville, and a few years before, the people who lived there had had a block party. A lot of families with kids lived on that street, so over time the event had become the unofficial start-of-summer party for kids, especially kids who went to MLK. Basically, if you knew someone who knew someone who knew someone who lived on or near Wilson, you were invited.

You were also invited if you were personal friends with the band, and I was really excited to see Sierra sing again. I hoped that the whole business with the banana slop wouldn't haunt me at the block party, but those hopes were not very high.

I spent a long time choosing the perfect outfit. I wanted a summery look that was festive but casual. After a lot of mixing and matching, I decided on a denim jumper dress with a polka-dot T-shirt underneath. To make my dress even more festive, I added glittery pin buttons that I had made myself. One of them was even an ice cream pin!

I looked at myself in the mirror and nodded, satisfied. I had a flash of inspiration: I should post about my custom pin buttons on my blog! But then I remembered. My blog was staying shut down until I posted an apology. And I wasn't feeling ready to post that apology yet.

Allie's dad dropped her off at my house at six thirty, and we walked over, because Wilson was pretty close to my street. Even a few blocks away, we could hear the sounds of kids' happy screams and music being played by a DJ.

"Look! There's a bouncy house this year!" I said, pointing.

"Fun!" Allie said. "Tanner was begging me to bring him, but I'm really glad Dad let me come by myself. He's taking Tanner to the movies instead."

I looked down at the plate of hummus and veggies my mom had made for me to bring. Since it was a block party, everybody contributed something. Allie had a box of cookies from Molly's. Thankfully, I no longer felt like crushing them.

"Let's go drop these off at the food table," I said.

"Sure," Allie agreed. "I'm hungry!"

We walked to the center of the block, where three big grills were smoking, tables were stacked with food, and coolers were full of sodas and bottled water. Nearby, Reagan was setting up her drum kit in front of two big speakers.

My stomach growled as I put down my plate.

We walked around the tables and piled food onto our plates. Pasta salad, tomatoes and mozzarella, crackers and cheese, potato salad—there was so much stuff! Allie and I took our plates over to a shady tree and started to chow down, watching people walk by. I was looking out for Sierra, and also for Ewan, I realized. I was really hoping to run into him. Then a terrible thought hit me. What if Ewan thought I was a horrible person because of the blog, like everybody else did? That would hurt.

As I was lost in that thought, three girls walked by. They were all wearing tank tops, denim shorts, and sandals. Each one had long, straight hair in the same style, but in a different shade. I vaguely recognized them as some girls from Allie's school that she and Colin called "the Mean Team." They stopped in front of us.

"Nice minidress, Tamiko," hissed the girl with sandy brown hair.

I froze. From her tone of voice, the girl wasn't complimenting me.

"What's that supposed to mean?" I asked.

Allie tugged on my arm. "Hey, let's just go."

The girl with dark brown hair—I thought her name was Palmer—said, "Minidress? You mean mini-MESS, don't you, Blair?" And all three girls cackled. I was beginning to understand the whole "Mean Team" thing.

"Now you know how it feels," added the blonde, and they laughed again and walked away.

I stared at them as they left, and then I realized that my mouth was open. I shut it. I looked down at my dress, which I thought was so cute. It was flowy with a flowery pattern and these bell sleeves that had been popular in the sixties but were hot again this summer.

"How do they even know me?" I asked.

"Everyone's been sharing your blog, Tamiko," Allie reminded me. "Your name is right on the site, so any kid who's on it can see your name."

"Those three girls are mean to everyone at your school, right?" I snapped. "They insult people every day. And I make one slightly-not-so-nice joke, and suddenly *I'm* the nasty one?"

"Don't let it get to you," Allie said. She held out her hand. "Here, give me your plate. I'm gonna find the garbage."

I obeyed and then frowned, thinking. I had been assuming that anyone following my blog would know me from school and understand my sense of humor. But putting myself publicly on the internet like that meant that I had to be my best self out there all the time, and not assume that people actually knew me. If I didn't, there would be consequences. Like people leaving mean comments. Or my being suspended from working on a website.

"Hey!" I yelled when I felt a yank on my ponytail. I spun around to see Ewan standing there, smiling.

"Whoa, chill!" He laughed. "I was just trying to get your attention. You looked deep in thought."

Then he moved in a little closer. "Although, word around town is that you've been kinda hostile lately."

I groaned. "Not you too? What am I, public enemy number one?"

Ewan laughed again. "Hey, I get your sense of humor," he said. "It's one of the things I like about you. You're honest. But other people may take things you say the wrong way."

"I know, I know!" I cried, exasperated. "I'm starting to wish I had never started the blog."

"Hey, don't say that," Ewan said. "I liked reading your blog. I was sad when you shut it down."

I was a little surprised, and happy, that Ewan had been reading my blog. I hadn't realized that people would actually miss it.

Then I felt someone staring at me. I turned around and saw two sixth graders from MLK looking at me and whispering. I groaned. "I think I *am* public enemy number one. Isn't there anybody who knew I was just joking?"

"I did," a quiet voice said behind me.

I turned to see who it was. It was Jodie!

"Jodie, you knew I was kidding?" I asked.

She nodded, her brown curls bouncing on her

shoulders. "I actually thought it was kind of funny," she said with a shy smile. "I mean, that sundae *was* banana slop! I knew it was bad when I posted it. I was kidding too!"

It hadn't even occurred to me that Jodie had known that her sundae was bad. Now that I thought about it, her post *was* pretty funny. She'd probably thought I'd make a silly comment about it and everybody would laugh. But I hadn't been able to tell it was a joke because, like Kai had said, it's hard to understand people's tones on the internet. I was starting to get a much better idea of why my response had caused so much trouble.

"I felt bad when all of those people got angry at you," Jodie continued. "I've been looking for you to tell you it was okay."

I hugged her. "Thank you so much," I said gratefully. "I'm sorry if I made you feel bad."

Jodie smiled at me. "It's okay," she said. "I was never mad! But I'd love for you to show me how to make a pretty banana split sometime."

"Definitely," I replied. And then it hit me. "That gives me an idea!"

Allie approached us. "Uh-oh. Another idea?"

"Trust me, this is a good one," I said. "But it's not

for tonight. Come on, let's go find Sierra!"

I said good-bye to Jodie and Ewan. Then Allie and I walked over to the band area. Reagan was tapping on her drums, Tessa was tuning her guitar, and Kasey was warming up on the keyboard. Sierra, meanwhile, was pacing back and forth.

She ran up and hugged us. "I was worried you weren't coming!"

"We wouldn't miss it!" I said.

Sierra scanned the crowd. "There are so many people here! It's crazy."

"You're not nervous, are you?" Allie asked.

"Of course I'm nervous!" Sierra replied. "I know this isn't our first gig, but it's definitely our biggest. What if people don't like us?"

"Hey, *I'm* the one people don't like today, so don't worry about it," I reminded her. "Besides, you guys are amazing."

"Right!" Allie agreed.

"Now get up there and sing your heart out!" I told her, giving her a push.

She laughed and joined the other Wildflowers. The girls huddled together for a moment and then took their places. Sierra grabbed the microphone.

"Hello, Wilson Street. We're the Wildflowers!"

Reagan counted off. "One, two, three, four!"

They launched into their first song, and a crowd gathered. Sierra sounded great! I took out my phone and began snapping pics of the band. If my plan worked, my blog would be up and running again soon, and I could get back to posting photos.

During their third song, Ewan came back over to Allie and me and just kind of stood next to us while we listened to the band. Then Colin walked up with Amanda and Eloise, two friendly girls from Allie's school. I noticed that Colin stood right next to Allie.

I looked at Allie and raised my eyebrows. She shrugged. Colin and Ewan could have been hanging out with anybody at this big block party, and they were hanging out with us. What did it all mean?

It doesn't have to mean anything, a little voice in my head told me. *Stop asking so many questions, and have fun!* Then I shouted, "Woo-hoo! Yay, Wildflowers!" at the top of my lungs. Ewan laughed, and I smiled at him.

I had a good feeling about everything—the Wildflowers, my blog, Molly's, and my friends!

CHAPTER ELEVEN

A PLAN

"You're up early, Tamiko," Mom said. "You've been getting up so late recently." Mom and Dad were in the kitchen. They both worked at the college nearby—Mom worked in the media office, and Dad was a professor—and usually drove in together. Dad was video-chatting with Grandpa Sato.

"Is that Tamiko?" I heard my grandfather say.

"Hi!" I greeted him.

"Let me see my Tamiko," Grandpa said, and Dad got up so that I could take the seat. "Good morning, Tamiko. Yesterday I spoke to Kai, and he told me what happened with your blog. Have you decided to apologize?"

Thanks, Kai, I thought. He will always throw me under the bus if it means he can be Grandpa's favorite.

"Yes," I told him. "I have a good idea about how to make things better. I'm going to take care of that today."

He smiled. "I knew you would do the right thing, Tamiko."

I gave the seat back to Dad and saw Mom staring at me with wide eyes.

"Okay, what did I miss?" she asked.

"It's not a super-big deal anymore," I began, and then I told her the story of what had happened, and my plan to make it right.

Mom shook her head. "I'm sorry, Tamiko. The internet is not always a positive place. I worry about the people who are writing negative comments on your site. But can I trust that you have it under control?"

"You can trust me," I said. "I'll let you know if they keep leaving mean comments, but I have a feeling it'll go away once I apologize."

"Okay," Mom said. "I've been so busy that I forgot to check in on your blog. I'm going to check in on it every day from now on, okay? Is there some way you can make me, like, an administrator? I know that adults can't log on to the site with their own accounts."

"I can forward my posts to you," I said. "As soon as I restart my blog. Just promise you won't cramp my style, okay?"

"When have I ever done that, my free-spirited daughter?" Mom asked.

I grinned. "Thanks, Ayumi!" I said, and then I grabbed a cereal bar and ran out before she could lecture me.

After school I sprinted to Molly's. The first part of my plan was to get to the store before the after-school rush so that I could talk to Mrs. S. privately. When I got there, I could see her wiping down tables, and the college students who usually helped her hadn't arrived yet. Perfect!

I coughed, and Mrs. S. looked up. "Tamiko? What are you doing here? Allie is at her dad's house," she said.

"Actually I came to talk with you. Is that okay?" I asked.

She nodded. "Sure. Let's sit down."

We sat at one of the round customer tables, which was a lot less stressful than talking to her over the top of an office desk.

"Is this about the website?" she asked.

I nodded. "I want to issue an apology on my blog, but I want it to be MY apology. I mean, I want to explain myself, but also offer up a peace offering."

Her eyes narrowed. "What kind of peace offering are we talking about?"

I took a deep breath. "I want to offer a Make Your Own Sundae demonstration at Molly's. For Jodie it will be free, but you could maybe charge a small fee for anyone else who would like to come. And they'd get to eat their creations afterward. What do you think?"

I crossed my fingers under the table. I knew it was a risky idea. We would have to shut down Molly's for an hour or two during the demonstration. Plus, even though we would make a little money on the demonstration fees, it might not be enough to cover the cost of the ice cream we'd be shelling out. Not to mention, there'd be prep before and cleanup afterward. But still, I knew it would make Jodie happy, and it might make other people like Molly's even more. I held my breath, waiting for Mrs. S. to answer me.

To my enormous relief, a big smile swept across her face. "I think that's a great idea," she said. "It will be a nice promotion, and it will get the reputation of

Molly's back on track as a nice, non-judgy place to visit."

I nodded. "That's exactly what I was thinking!"

"I don't even think we should charge people anything for the sundae-making class," she said. "How about we do this: Why don't you write up a draft of your apology and the invitation to the demonstration? Show it to me, and we'll get moving on your idea. This demonstration could be really fun. Maybe we'll even film it and post it on the web page when it's over."

"Great idea, Mrs. S.!" I said. "I hadn't thought of that!"

Mrs. S. stood up. "Thanks, Tamiko. I appreciate that you're trying to make this right."

"I have to," I said. "I love Molly's!"

I left the shop feeling excited about the plan. I just needed one more thing to make it work. I stopped at the food market on Ocean Avenue. I went to the banana bin and dug to the bottom until I found a rotten banana covered with brown spots. The guy at the checkout gave me a weird look when I bought it.

"Even rotten bananas need love," I told him, which did not change the weird look on his face one bit.

Then I went home, took the banana to my room, and took a photo of it. Then I started to type what had been rolling around in my head. I started with the title: "I Am a Bad Banana!"

"Recently I made fun of a sundae created by a Molly's customer. It was a silly remark, and I meant no harm. And luckily, the person the comment was meant for knew I was joking. But a lot of people didn't, and I apologize to you all.

"I also want to do something more. I'd like to offer a free demonstration at Molly's on how to make a classic banana split. Pretty to look at, but also, more important, delicious to eat. (And made with beautiful, yellow bananas!) Once your banana split is completed, you'll get to eat your masterpiece! If you're interested, send an e-mail to Molly's today. Seating is limited."

Then I added a photo of the beautiful banana split that Allie had made for my photo shoot.

I saved the post as a draft and e-mailed it to Mrs. S. with some ideas for dates and times when we could do it. I knew she was working, but I anxiously kept checking my e-mail to see if she had replied.

To pass the time, I tried to finish a project I'd

been working on—gluing alphabet tiles from a word game onto an old purse. If I was going to keep doing the blog, I'd need to keep up with my projects. I had trouble deciding on what words to make, though.

"FASHION"? Predictable.

"LOVE"? Corny.

"BANANA"? I really needed to stop thinking about bananas!

Fortunately, Mrs. S. e-mailed me back before dinnertime.

"This is perfect, Tamiko! Go ahead and upload the apology to your blog, and I'll upload the demonstration announcement to the Molly's website."

That message made me happy and also a little sad, because it reminded me that I was suspended from the Molly's website. One step at a time, I guess. I quickly uploaded the new post.

"Set Your Blog to Live?" the screen prompted.

I hit the Yes button confidently. Then I texted Sierra and Allie.

The blog is back up. And there's a little surprise. ☽ ♥

?????, Allie texted back, but then she must have checked it out, because I saw that the blog had gotten a new view. A second later she texted, ♥ ♥ ♥

You are not a bad banana! ☺, Sierra texted me.

I asked my friends if they would help out during the demonstration, and they said yes! I grinned. I knew that things were 100 percent cool with Allie and Sierra. Now I just had to find out what the rest of the world thought.

I turned back to my purse project and made a few more words with the tiles.

"TRUTH"? Too preachy.

"FREEDOM"? What did that have to do with a purse?

"STUFF"? Definitely more purselike. Not bad.

I checked my blog. Some comments were starting to come in.

"Sounds like fun!"

"Mmmm, banana splits!"

Nothing about forgiving me or anything, but that was cool. At least the comments had stopped being mean!

Then I saw a comment from Jodie. "Thanks, Tamiko! I'll be there!"

That one made me happy. Happy that Jodie hadn't been hurt by my comment, and also happy that maybe other people would see her comment from today and stop dogging me for being mean to her.

Then I checked the announcement about the demonstration on the Molly's website (as a visitor, not an admin). That had comments too!

"Hooray for ice cream!"

"I signed up. Yay!"

That was a good sign that the demonstration would be filled up. I felt so relieved that my banana mess didn't seem to be hurting Molly's business. I just hoped that Mrs. S. wasn't still disappointed in me.

About an hour later I got an e-mail from Mrs. S.

"All slots filled! Great idea, Tamiko."

I couldn't believe it! The demo had filled up so fast! I was so excited that I reread Mrs. S.'s e-mail over and over again.

My blog was up and running, people were excited about the demonstration, and no one was mad at me anymore.

It felt good to be the queen of social media again.

CHAPTER TWELVE
A SWEET ENDING

"Welcome to the first ever Molly's sundae-making demonstration!" I announced.

It was a sunny Saturday morning. Bayville was packed with beachgoers, and Molly's Ice Cream was closed for a banana-split-making demonstration.

Kai was with me. I'd asked him to get a video of the demonstration that we could put on the Molly's website, and he'd agreed—if I paid him ten bucks. I'd almost argued with him, because I was pretty much broke after all the stuff I'd bought for my blog photo shoots. But I wanted to do this right for Mrs. S., so I'd said yes. Also, I had acted ungrateful when he'd told me to post an apology on my blog, and that had turned out to be good advice. So I felt like I owed him one (or ten).

Mrs. S. had decided on fifteen people for the demonstration, which seemed manageable. Jodie was there with two of her friends. Some of our regular customers were there: two white-haired ladies who came every Wednesday at the same time and ordered vanilla cones, and a mom who was there almost every day with her two little boys. Allie's friends Eloise and Amanda had shown up too. And there were a few people I didn't recognize. We'd told everyone to take a seat at one of the tables.

"Those boys are going to make such a mess!" Allie had whispered to me before we'd started.

"It will be fine," I'd promised her. Allie, Sierra, and I had come in early to set up the demonstration, and I was pretty confident it would be a success.

"Today we're going to make a banana split with a Molly's twist," I began. "First of all, can anyone guess the year that banana splits were invented?"

The mom raised her hand. "1955?" she asked.

"It would have to be earlier than that, dear," said one of the white-haired ladies. "I remember eating them when I was a little girl at my uncle's soda shop."

"You're right, it was earlier than 1955," I said. "It was actually 1904. A guy named David Strickler worked at a soda fountain at a pharmacy in Pennsylvania. He liked to experiment with making different sundaes, and he came up with the banana split. Word got around, and it became popular all over, which is pretty amazing, considering that was before the internet was invented."

"I was also invented before the internet," the same white-haired lady said, and everybody laughed.

"Please put on the plastic gloves we've provided, and then pick up the boat-shaped bowl in front of you. That's the traditional bowl used for a banana split," I informed them. "The first thing that goes in is three scoops of ice cream. The traditional flavors are chocolate, vanilla, and strawberry, but here at Molly's we like to use the Banana Pudding flavor in place of the vanilla. Allie is going to demonstrate how to scoop, and then we can start filling our bowls."

I turned to Allie. We had put three tubs of ice cream on one of the long tables, so people didn't have to go behind the counter to get it. We had the toppings set up next to them.

"The first thing you need to get a nice, round scoop is a glass of hot water," she said, and she dipped the metal ice cream scoop into it. "This will help you get the ice cream out more easily. It also helps if you take your ice cream out of the freezer for a few minutes to soften it up. We've done that today, but otherwise our ice cream is always frozen hard when we scoop it."

She plunged the scoop into the tub of chocolate ice cream. "Now here's a trick. Try to make an S shape as you scoop, twisting your wrist like this. That helps you form the ice cream into a ball."

She demonstrated, and then she plopped the scoop of chocolate into her boat. "See?"

The white-haired ladies clapped. The little boys started jumping up and down.

"Can we try? Can we try?" they yelled.

"Yes, line up and grab a scoop," I instructed. (Mrs. S. had researched it, and for food safety reasons, every group needed their own scoop. But we had enough in the shop, so that was okay.) "Dip your scoop into the water before you do each new ice cream ball."

Jodie and her friends lined up first. Jodie picked up the scoop and tentatively dug it into the tub of ice cream.

"Get it in there," Allie coached her. "You want to submerge the round part of the scoop all the way."

Jodie nodded and then made an S shape as she scooped. A perfect round ball of chocolate plopped into her bowl.

"Perfect!" I said, and she gave me a big smile.

Everybody scooped their ice cream, and Allie helped the two little boys so that they made perfect scoops too, which made them really happy.

"Now we nestle a sliced banana half on each side of the ice cream, like this," I said, demonstrating. Everybody moved down the line, adding their bananas.

"And now comes the fun part—toppings," I said. "The lovely Sierra is going to show us how it's done."

"Hey, you're the singer for the Wildflowers!" a teenage girl exclaimed, and Sierra blushed a little.

"That's me," she said. "But today I'm making banana splits, not singing."

I narrated as Sierra topped the sundae that Allie and I had started.

"For the banana split you'll need three sauces: chocolate syrup, strawberry sauce, and caramel sauce," I said. "You can find all of these in any supermarket. You can see that Sierra is using a small spoon, and she is carefully drizzling the sauces, one at a time, over the ice cream. Each scoop should have all of the sauces on it when you're done. And don't put too much, or it will become soupy."

The little boys needed some extra attention during the topping phase, and there was definitely some spillage. Allie swooped in with some wet wipes and cleaned the sauces off the boys' arms, earning a grateful smile from their mom.

"After the sauces come the crushed nuts," I said. "We use walnuts here, but you could use any nuts you want. Or leave the nuts off altogether, if you're allergic."

After everyone was done with the nuts, Sierra picked up a whipped cream canister.

"A neat way to do this is to squirt a little rosette onto each of the scoops," I said as Sierra demonstrated. "But if you love whipped cream, you can go a little crazy."

On cue, Sierra started to make the whipped cream piles higher.

Everyone took turns with the whipped cream. When it was the little boys' turn, I leaned closer to them. "The whipped cream stays on the ice cream. Got it?"

They nodded, eager to please, and were both very careful when applying their whipped cream. I flashed a smile at Allie.

"The final touch is usually a cherry on top," I said, "but here at Molly's we add one more thing. A sprinkle of happy!"

Sierra put a cherry on top of our sample sundae, and I added a shower of rainbow sprinkles. Everybody clapped, and Kai came in with his camera to get a close-up.

"Now you know how to make a perfect banana split," I said. "But remember, don't be afraid to experiment! Try different flavors and toppings and combinations at home. It might not turn out to be the perfect banana split, but it would be *your* unique creation!"

Jodie smiled warmly at me. I think she understood what I was talking about.

"Now here's the best part," I said. "It's time to eat!"

Everyone began to eat. Some people were taking pictures of their sundaes.

"Hashtag Molly's Ice Cream!" I shouted.

Mrs. S., who had been watching the whole time, approached me.

"This was very successful, Tamiko," she said. "Thank you so much."

"Kai's going to edit the footage later today," I said.

"I'll have him send it to you so you can put it up on the website."

"You can do that yourself, Tamiko," she said.

Had I heard her right? "You mean . . ."

She nodded. "You handled this very professionally today. I trust that you will continue to act professionally as the social media director for Molly's. If you still want to do it?"

"YES!" I shrieked. "Thank you! I won't let you down!"

Mrs. S. turned to Allie and Sierra. "Daphne and Rashid are coming in a few minutes to start their shift. If you wouldn't mind cleaning up, I'll open the shop."

"No problem!" Allie said, and we all pitched in to put away the ice cream and the toppings. Daphne and Rashid showed up, and Mrs. S. opened the shop.

"So, does this all mean that you're going to keep posting on your blog?" Sierra asked.

"Definitely," I said. I still had so many ideas and things I wanted to share with the world. "But I don't think I'll pressure myself to post that often. That way I can be more thoughtful about what I write."

Allie nodded approvingly. "We'll always be your number one readers!" she said.

"Thanks," I said, and smiled. "So, what are you both doing for the rest of today?"

"I'm volunteering at the library today," Allie said. "I signed up for a few hours a week, until camp starts."

"I'm going to the beach with my family," Sierra said. "Want to come?"

"Sure, maybe," I said. It was a beautiful day, but I had some big plans for my next blog post that I wanted to start on.

The bell on the door tinkled, and Ewan walked in. Allie and Sierra raised their eyebrows at me and then walked away from me as Ewan approached.

"I guess I'm too late for the banana split thing?" he asked.

I nodded. "Yeah, you had to sign up in advance," I said.

"I just saw it on your blog," he said. "And a banana split sounded so good that I thought I'd come down."

"You can still get one," I told him, nodding to the counter.

He looked around at the banana splits that everyone was eating. "Wow, they're pretty big. If I get one, will you share it with me?"

"Uh . . . ," I said. My hands began to sweat. Wasn't sharing a sundae with someone sort of . . . romantic? Behind me I swore I heard Allie and Sierra giggle.

"Sure," I declared to Ewan. Then I turned around to face my friends. "Allie and Sierra can help us eat it too!"

"Okay," Ewan replied. I might have detected a hint of disappointment in his voice, but I pretended not to hear it.

We walked up to the counter, and Ewan ordered a banana split from Daphne. I nervously narrated as Daphne was making it.

"Well, since you missed the demonstration, I can tell you how it's done," I interjected. "See how Daphne is making that S shape? . . . Okay, now she's evenly drizzling the chocolate sauce. . . ."

Ewan paid for the sundae and we got four spoons and headed to one of the round tables. I could feel Allie and Sierra staring at me, confused. I called out to them. "Seriously? You're going to pass up on an opportunity to eat a banana split?"

That made both of them grin, and they joined Ewan and me at the table.

Ewan looked down at the banana split. "Wow,

those are perfectly round scoops," he said. "I'm going to have to try that S-shaped trick at home."

"Practice makes perfect!" Sierra said.

I smiled at him gratefully, plucked the cherry off the top of the sundae, and popped it into my mouth.

"Hey, aren't you supposed to eat that last?" he asked.

"I was born to break the rules," I answered. It sounded corny as soon as I said it, but everyone laughed. I picked up my spoon and dug into the ice cream.

That banana split was sweet and delicious. Hanging out with my Sprinkle Sundays sisters *and* Ewan was pretty sweet too. So was being able to run the Molly's website again.

I suddenly knew the perfect word to make with my alphabet tiles.

"SWEET"!

DON'T MISS BOOK 9:

SUGAR, SPICE, AND SPRINKLES

I hurried down the school hallway, balancing a large Tupperware container, my reusable lunch bag, my backpack, and a separate small duffel bag that held notes, sheet music, and a granola bar for my band practice later. When you participated in as many activities as I did, you needed to be prepared. It didn't hurt to bring a few snacks, either.

That day's student council meeting had been pushed back twice because of me and my other commitments, like rehearsals with my amazing band, the Wildflowers; my soccer and softball team practices; and my weekly shifts at Molly's, the best ice cream parlor in town, where I worked with my two best friends every Sunday.

Student council was important to me too, though. I loved being the secretary and taking notes and getting to weigh in and vote on upcoming school events and fund-raisers. I was helping to make my school a more fun and friendlier place. What could be better?

So, to make sure everyone on the council knew how much it meant to me that they'd moved the meeting around (twice), I'd spent some time the day before baking cookies to bring to the meeting. People appreciated cookies, especially after school when you were starving.

I broke into a jog as room 215B came into sight. Then I *whooshed* through the door, and all of my bags and packages banged and slapped against the doorframe and desks as I made my way to the big table by the windows. Let's just say my entrance was loud, even for me.

Everyone turned to see if a herd of elephants was coming, and then made faces like, *Oh, it's not elephants, it's just Sierra.* The four student council members (besides me) were already there, even though it was only 3:13 and the school bell had just rung at 3:10. How had they all gotten there so fast? I had practically run from my locker, and it was only one floor down.

Maybe I needed roller skates.

"Hello, everyone!" I said cheerfully. I plopped the large Tupperware container onto the table and began depositing my other bags into a chair. "Help yourselves!"

"Ooooh, what's in here?" asked Claire Bright, sliding her thumb under the corner of the Tupperware lid. Claire was in eighth grade and was president of the student council. She worked *very* hard on all council business, and always wanted everything to be just right. "Wow, Sierra. Really, wow! You made *emoji cookies*?"

She pulled one out and held it up to show everyone. I beamed. What had started out as making plain old sugar cookies (round ones—I didn't even use a cookie cutter because I didn't have time for the dough to chill and set) had become much more interesting when I'd discovered we had a lot of yellow food dye. So I'd whipped up some icing and given all the cookies yellow faces, then had had a blast adding eyes and mouths and different common emoji expressions. Even my identical twin sister, Isa, who basically did the opposite of everything I did and would say she didn't like something just because *I* liked it, had stopped by the kitchen to admire them. She had even gotten into the spirit of things and decorated a few *Yuck!* faces with tongues sticking out.

"These are *awesome*," said Lee Murphy, our treasurer and resident council grump, biting into a well-chosen frowny face.

Hanna Okoye (sixth-grade rep who recently joined the student council) and Vikram Kapoor (vice president) both nodded in agreement and reached into the Tupperware to grab a few for themselves. I waited until everyone had a cookie before choosing a toothy smiley face for myself.

Everyone was munching and smiling, and I could tell it was going to be a good meeting.

Claire, finishing her third cookie, called the meeting to order. "First order of business—let's all thank Sierra for being so nice and bringing us these awesome cookies! I guess it made this meeting worth the wait."

Everyone clapped, and I gave a silly half bow.

"Really, Sierra—you are just soooo nice," Claire said. "Someone asked me the other day about you, and I said Sierra is a *sweetheart*."

Hanna, who tended to be a bit shy in meetings

because she was the only sixth grader, said, "Yeah, you are so sweet, Sierra."

"And a good baker, too," said Lee, polishing off his fourth or fifth cookie. "Sweet Sierra."

I was starting to feel a little self-conscious now, like they were describing a cookie, not me. So I jumped right into reading the minutes from the previous meeting, to change the subject.

"We need to plan Spirit Week," I read from my notes, "which includes making a plan for promo materials and an assembly, and also deciding on the themes for the week."

"I love Spirit Week," said Claire. "It's the best! And since it's my last year here at MLK, I want to make sure we do an awesome job, okay?"

"Of course!" I said. "I love Spirit Week too!"

Hanna and the others quickly agreed, and we started brainstorming ideas. We made a list of how many posters we'd need, who was going to make them, and the basics of what they would look like and say. Then we started discussing our assembly, which had mostly been arranged for us, and would include a speaker who was an alum of the school giving a speech entitled Achieving Success under Stress.

I almost felt like *I* could give that speech, since most of the time I was running from one thing to the next, trying to make it all work and be successful. I giggled to myself, thinking how hard my two best friends, Allie Shear and Tamiko Sato, would laugh if I told them I was going to give that speech. They always teased me about my overly busy schedule, and both of them preferred to live life on the slower, calmer side.

"Why are you laughing, Sierra?" asked Lee. "You don't like the red–and–gold idea?"

"Huh?" I said, not realizing I'd tuned out for a moment. I checked my notes, which I'd been taking very diligently, and saw that Lee had suggested having a Red and Gold Day for one of our spirit dress–up days, in honor of our school colors.

"I wasn't laughing at that!" I replied hastily. "I was just thinking of how great Spirit Week is going to be, and it made me happy, so I guess I . . . just happy–laughed." I smiled and shrugged sheepishly, realizing I sounded a little kooky, but better that than admitting I'd been daydreaming and thinking of something else.

Vikram shook his head. "So happy and sweet! You're like a baby bird, Sierra."

I didn't really see how I was similar to a baby bird, but since he seemed to mean it as a compliment, I said nothing and went back to taking notes.

"Do we have some ideas for the other four days of the week?" I asked. "Other than Red and Gold Day, I mean?"

Everyone started shouting out ideas, and I wrote them down as fast as I could.

Crazy Hair Day
Inside Out Day
Pajama Day
Sports Jersey Day
Hawaiian Day
Favorite Decade Day
Heroes vs. Villains Day
Favorite Movie Day
Eighties Day

We were coming up with so many ideas that I didn't know how we'd choose just five total. There were endless possibilities for Spirit Week, which was why it was fun every year, and why I was glad to be on the student council and able to help make these decisions!

I grabbed a second cookie for myself and kept jotting down notes, until the clock read four fifteen.

"Hey, guys, I'm sorry to do this but I have to leave a little early—I've got a band practice now and I couldn't push it until later. . . ." I hated feeling guilty when I had to leave one thing to go to another, but with my schedule, it happened fairly often.

"It's okay, Sierra," Claire said. "We understand, and I think we've had a really productive meeting today. But leave these delicious cookies behind, will you?"

I had planned to take the extras for my band, but I couldn't say no when Claire was being so nice about me leaving early. So I just smiled and said, "Of course! Enjoy. And I can't wait for Spirit Week! We're going to have so much fun!"

"Bye, Sierra," said Hanna in her soft voice.

I waved to everyone and set off for my band-mate Reagan's house, feeling lighter without the heavy Tupperware container. I couldn't wait to tell the band some of the ideas we'd come up with for Spirit Week.

Then another idea occurred to me. What about a Rock 'n' Roll Day? That would be fun and easy to do—just dress like your favorite rock star! Spirit

Week was always the best week of the year. And I'd gotten to help plan it *and* go spend time with my band.

"Who says Mondays are terrible?" I asked myself as I hiked down the school driveway and headed in the direction of Reagan's house. "If you ask me, I think they're pretty sweet."

"It's slow in here today," said Tamiko, looking at the clock on the wall of Molly's Ice Cream parlor. "We've only had, like, six customers. Maybe I should post a special on social media. Allie, quick! Come up with something photogenic." She gestured frantically at Allie, as if urging her to put out a fire.

Allie and I exchanged a look. Tamiko was terrific with social media and getting customers in the door. But she could also be a *little* too blunt and bossy sometimes without meaning to. I winked at Allie, and she gave me a knowing smile back.

"Ooo-kay," Allie said slowly. "Well, it's Sunday, so how about something like a Sweet End to the Weekend cone? It could be three or four different scoops, with a piece of candy hidden at the bottom of the cone to find at the end—"

Tamiko clapped her hands together excitedly, and said, "Yes! Make it now! I'll post it and we'll get some people in here."

Allie got to work while I grabbed her phone to turn up the music that was playing on the speakers. I looked forward to Sundays every week, because every Sunday I got to scoop ice cream and hang out with my two best friends.

Well, technically, I didn't do very much of the scooping. When the three of us worked together, Allie was the super-scooper, creating beautiful, edible works of art; Tamiko was the marketing maven, often dreaming up delicious, original, *personal* concoctions for customers on the spot; and I was the register runner, because I could do math really fast in my head. I never got flustered if the register jammed or when four different people were shoving money into my hands and waiting for their change.

We were a great team, thanks to years of being such good friends.

Allie made the new cone, and Tamiko posted it online. Not one second later, a customer walked into the shop. It was as if we'd asked a genie for a wish. Tamiko winked at me, and we all scooted into our positions.

The customer was a mom with a young toddler. The woman's hair was piled into a messy bun on top of her head, with stray pieces flying every which way. Her scarf was askew, and her purse gaped open, stuffed with a sippy cup, a plastic baggie of snacks, and what looked like a small blanket. She seemed exhausted. I felt tired just looking at her.

Her toddler was red-faced and kept yanking on her arm. "NO, NO, NO, NO, NO, NO," he was yelling, and he even stamped his foot a few times. "I don't *WANNA*."

"Hello!" Allie said cheerfully. "Welcome to Molly's, where all of our ice creams are homemade right here in the store. What can we get you? We've got a special today—a Sweet End to the Weekend cone, which has a hidden surprise at the bottom."

The woman scanned the containers of ice cream, and said, "Um, thanks, but I'll just have a double scoop of Coffee and Doughnuts ice cream for me, and a cup of the Cake Batter for my son. Oh, and do you have a cup of coffee to go with the coffee ice cream?"

"We sure do," I said, and Tamiko scrambled to get it ready for her.

"Black. Hot. Extra strong, please," the woman said. I had a feeling that what this woman really needed was a nap.

Allie got to work on the order and Tamiko snapped a lid onto the coffee while I rang it all up. Allie handed over the finished cone and cup of ice cream, which were both works of art, as always. She made sure her scoops were perfectly round and full. After all, Molly's was her mother's store, and their family needed it to be as successful as possible.

But as soon as the little boy took his cup of ice cream, he started stamping his feet again and yelling, *"I said I wanted BLUE ICE CREAM!"* He quickly flipped over the cup so that the scoops fell onto the floor at his feet.

The mother looked like she was going to lose it. She put her hand to her forehead, closing her eyes and sighing deeply.

Allie, Tamiko, and I exchanged a look. We'd never had a kid dump ice cream onto the floor before. Most kids ate it so fast, there wasn't even time for drips.

"Oh, that's no problem at all," I said brightly.

"Really! Allie will get him a fresh cup of something uh . . . blue, on the house, and I'll clean up the mess."

"Really?" asked the woman.

"Really," said Allie. And I knew she didn't mind me offering it on the house just this once. She and her mother always wanted every customer to leave happy, and I felt it was my job to make sure that happened.

I hurried to get the mop and clean up the mess as Allie made him a cup of Blueberry Wonder, which was more purple than blue, but it was the closest thing we had. As she was placing the cup on the counter, I reached into the sprinkles bin and pulled out a handful of pale blue sprinkles. I arranged them on the top of the scoop in a smiley face, and said, "Here's a *blue* sprinkle of happy to go with your *blue* ice cream."

The toddler's face lit up, and so did his mother's. "Thank you," she said. "You are so sweet! We'll definitely come back again."

"Yay!" said Tamiko as they left. "Another happy customer. You really are the nicest, Sierra. I mean, Allie and I are both nice too—don't get me wrong—but you are just *extra* nice."

"So true," said Allie, putting her arm around my

shoulders and giving me a squeeze. "You're the nicest person I know. I'm so glad you're my friend."

"Me too," I said, feeling pleased, but also slightly uncomfortable at all the praise. I'd just done what anyone would have done, right?

To change the subject I said, "I forgot to tell you about my student council meeting the other day. We started coming up with ideas for Spirit Week!"

"YES!" Tamiko jumped up and down a few times. "Spirit Week is my *jam*! I get to make so many great outfits!"

Tamiko loved any excuse to make, create, glue—you name it. Her room and her wardrobe were all completely unique and custom.

"Remember Spirit Week in sixth grade?" asked Allie, sounding wistful. "I was still at MLK, and we had Twin Day, and the three of us decided to go as triplets?" Allie, Tamiko, and I used to all go to the same school—Martin Luther King Middle School—but Allie switched to Vista Green School after her parents got divorced.

"And the best part was that Sierra actually *has* a twin but dressed up with us anyway!" added Tamiko.

I smiled. That had been a great day. "It's not like

Isa would have agreed to dress identically with me anyway," I reminded them. "She'd already started her all-black phase by then."

"True, but you could have dressed like *her*," Allie said.

Tamiko nodded.

I was quiet for a minute, dismayed that I hadn't thought of that. It had never occurred to me that I could have offered to wear Isa's style of clothes, because to me they looked so . . . sad.

"You're right," I said. "I guess I could have dressed like Isa."

"Back to this year, though," said Tamiko. "What's the plan for the themes? I want to get my glue gun warmed up and ready to go."

"We're still brainstorming," I told her. "So if you guys have ideas, don't be shy!"

Immediately Allie said, "Well, I'd vote for Favorite Book Characters Day, obviously."

I smiled. It was such an Allie suggestion, because Allie loved to read, and even had her own column called Get the Scoop in her school's newspaper, where she recommended books and the best flavor of ice cream to enjoy while reading each one.

"Book characters! That's perfect—I'll mention it."

"How about a DIY Day?" Tamiko suggested. "Everyone can decorate their own T-shirt with fabric paints and pens at school."

"Oooh, I love that one too." I grabbed my phone and typed the suggestions into my notes section, to make sure I'd remember them for the next student council meeting. "You're both really brilliant, you know."

"The Sprinkle Sundays sisters never disappoint," Tamiko joked, using the special name we had for ourselves.

"That's for sure," said Allie. "Hey, look! A soccer team is coming in. To your stations, ladies!"

Things got busy then for a while and we didn't have much chance to talk. At the end of our shift, Allie's mom, Mrs. Shear, called us all into the back room (or backstage, as she referred to it) for one of the best parts of our job—taste-testing.

"I've been working on this one for more than two weeks," Mrs. Shear said, giving us each a spoonful of smooth dark brown ice cream. "It's called Chocolate Chili. A little different from my usual flavors, so let me know what you think. And please be honest!"

Allie went first. "Wow, Mom. This is amazing! I've never had ice cream that has, you know, a *kick* to it! It's so neat!"

Tamiko tried it next and agreed. "This is awesome, Mrs. S.! It's very refreshing to mix up something traditionally sweet by adding the hot chili spice."

I went last. After so much praise from my friends, I couldn't wait to taste it. But the second the ice cream hit my tongue, I was confused, and not in a good way. It didn't taste *bad*, it just . . . didn't taste like ice cream. I loved the delicious sweet chocolate but I didn't like the peppery heat of the chili spice. Wasn't ice cream supposed to be just sweet? Why go and ruin it with spices?

Mrs. Shear was watching me anxiously, as were Tamiko and Allie. They wanted to know what I thought.

"Well?" asked Mrs. Shear. "Tell me the truth, Sierra. I value your opinion."

"It's great!" I said, making sure to sound convincing. "Really good." Mrs. Shear sighed with relief, and Allie beamed. I knew she was proud of her mother for opening this store and coming up with so many unique and interesting homemade flavors.

If Allie and Tamiko liked the Chocolate Chili flavor, then other customers might too. It wasn't like I was some kind of ice cream expert. What did I know? I was the register runner, not the taste buds queen.

And anyway, I didn't want to hurt Mrs. Shear's feelings by telling her it didn't really taste like ice cream to me. That wouldn't be nice at all, and I was always nice.

Walking in the front door of my house, I smelled something amazing. It had to be my dad's cooking.

I dropped my bags and shoes in one of the few empty spots by the front door, and hurried past the piles of clutter in the hallway: magazines, the odd box or two, a coatrack, a basket of shoes. I loved that my family lived comfortably in our clutter. Well, most of us, anyway. Isa's room was always as neat as a pin, but the rest of us plopped stuff any old place and it worked just fine.

From the kitchen doorway I saw my dad opening the oven door and pulling out a large roasting pan full of delicious-looking meat.

"Papi?" I said. "Do I smell carne con papas?"

Even though I hadn't enjoyed Mrs. Shear's spicy ice cream, my mouth was already watering for my father's tasty meat-and-potato dish. My parents had been born in Cuba, and my father was a fantastic chef of Cuban food. That was where spice belonged, in my opinion.

"*Sí*, Sierra!" my father replied. "It is. I made it just for you."

The table was already set for four, and my mother was helping to plate the food. My stomach grumbled just looking at all the yummy things my dad had made. He and my mother were both veterinarians and ran a veterinary clinic together, working long hours most days of the week. However, the hospital was closed on Sundays, so my dad liked to make a big family meal and have lots of leftovers for the week. I liked it too.

My mom walked over and kissed me on the head. "Sit down. We're ready."

Isa was already at the table in a black hooded sweatshirt, her head bent as she read a book. Isa loved books as much as Allie did, so you'd think they'd still be friends. But Isa had stopped hanging out with Allie and Tamiko (and me) a year or two before, even though when we were younger, they'd all gotten along fine. Isa still said hi when my friends came over to see me, but she wouldn't join us for a movie, go to the mall together, or even sit and have a snack with us.

"*Hola*, Isa," I said.

"Hey," she replied, not lifting her eyes.

We all sat down and took turns talking about our day. Sunday dinners were a big deal at our house, since during the week Isa or I might be out somewhere and miss dinner, and one of our parents often stayed late at the vet clinic to see sick patients.

"This is delicious, Papi," I said, digging into my food. Isa mumbled her agreement. "Even better than usual."

"*Gracias*. How were things at Molly's today, Sierra?"

"Good! Mrs. Shear is thinking of introducing a new ice cream flavor with some spice in it—something really different. I taste-tested it this afternoon—Chocolate Chili."

My mom smiled. "What a great idea! I bet I'd love it."

"Allie and Tamiko both did. I thought it was more confusing than good."

"But you love spice," said my mom.

"I know, but ice cream is a dessert! It's supposed to be sweet. I do love spicy Cuban food, but it's a main course. I think things should be what they're supposed to be."

My dad shook his head. "Sometimes. But it's okay to mix it up now and then. We're not all just one thing, you know. Like I'm a vet, but also a wonderful chef, as you like to tell me."

"I guess so," I mumbled. Inside, though, I disagreed. I liked to know what things were, and I liked them to be consistent.

"Tell us what you have going on this week," my mom said. "I want to make sure we have our schedules laid out and synced up."

"I have a few student council meetings after school. We've started planning for Spirit Week," I told everyone. I went on to explain some of our ideas and the plans we were making. I was hoping Isa would join in the conversation, since it was about her school too, but I could tell by the way her head was bent sharply as she ate that she'd snuck her book beneath the table and was reading it in her lap.

"Allie and Tamiko suggested Favorite Book

Characters Day and DIY Day," I said.

My dad laughed and said, "That sounds just like them. But what would *your* choice be?"

"I don't know. I like all of them!" I replied.

"How about Twin Day?" my mom suggested. "That would be perfect for you girls. It was so much fun dressing you two in matching outfits when you were little. The same outfit, but in different colors. You both loved it."

My mom beamed as I glanced nervously over at Isa to see what she'd think of the idea.

"Isa?" my dad said. "Pull your nose out of your book, *por favor*. What do you think?"

Isa lifted her head slightly and shrugged, not looking at me. "Sure. They could do a Twin Day. But Sierra would choose to dress up with Tamiko and Allie—just like she did last year. The days of Sierra and me looking alike are *looooooong* gone." Then she went back to reading the book in her lap.

My mom and dad both looked at me questioningly. I nodded, letting them know that yes, I had dressed up with Tamiko and Allie on Twin Day the year before.

My mom looked down, clearly disappointed.

I felt awful. At the time, Isa had said she'd rather drop dead than dress up with me. But I knew Isa well enough to know that her words didn't always match her feelings, and I should have been more thoughtful. Her tone just now had made it clear that she was still holding that Twin Day against me.

I felt terrible—like a disloyal twin. No matter what was going on with Isa and me, I never, ever wanted to hurt her feelings.

Noticing the awkward silence, Papi tried to smooth things over by passing the food around again. "I'm really looking forward to your soccer game on Thursday," he said to Isa. "The semifinals! We'll all be there to cheer you on."

Oh no. No, no, no, no! I had completely forgotten about Isa's game. She played on a supercompetitive all-boys travel team (not the regular seventh-grade girls' team I was on at school), and they'd made it to the regional semifinals. And the game was this week.

"Shoot!" I burst out. "Student council booked another meeting for this Thursday, and I said I would be there."

Isa snorted. "Of course you did. You always have an excuse to miss my games. Thanks a bunch, Sisi."

I bristled. Maybe I'd missed a few of her regular games, but it wasn't like she came to all of mine. And anyway, I wouldn't miss her big game this week—I would never do that!

"I'll be there," I said. "I just need to reschedule the meeting, that's all."

I sounded confident, but in the back of my mind I was already worried about having to ask to move another meeting, so soon after the last one. But I would have to make things work.

"Can I be excused, *por favor*?" Isa asked, standing up and tucking her book into the front pocket of her oversize sweatshirt.

My mom nodded, and Isa stomped off. Her bedroom door shut loudly enough that we knew she was annoyed, but not loudly enough to be a slam, because my parents hated slammed doors.

My parents looked at me, and I could tell they were both disappointed that I hadn't dressed up with Isa for Twin Day the year before, and that I'd forgotten about Isa's game. I knew they relied on me to be the one who was easy to talk to and always smoothed the waters, especially since Isa had become so distant in the previous year.

But I wasn't perfect. And anyway, Tamiko and Allie were my Sprinkle Sundays sisters! My best friends for life. We'd had *fun* dressing up together. And wasn't Spirit Week supposed to be fun?

My dad changed the subject to the vet clinic as we finished dinner, and I offered to do the dishes afterward since I felt so bad. When I was done, I texted Tamiko:

If we did Twin Day again this year, would you want to dress up together?

She immediately replied: Duh! We're Sprinkle Sundays sisters forever!

I slid the phone back into my skirt pocket and headed upstairs. I had a lot of work to do. First I needed to get the council to agree to move Thursday's meeting, and then I had to make sure we had so many great ideas for this year's Spirit Week that we *definitely* wouldn't be choosing Twin Day.

This identical twin couldn't handle it.

Looking for another great book?
Find it
IN THE MIDDLE.

Fun, fantastic books for kids
in the in-be**TWEEN** age.

IntheMiddleBooks.com

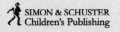 SIMON & SCHUSTER
Children's Publishing   **f** /SimonKids   🐦 @SimonKids

sew zoey

Zoey's clothing design blog puts her on the A-list in the fashion world . . . but when it comes to school, will she be teased, or will she be a trendsetter? Find out in the Sew Zoey series:

EBOOK EDITIONS ALSO AVAILABLE
SewZoeyBooks.com • Published by Simon Spotlight • Kids.SimonandSchuster.com